'You don't g
very reluctan
to soften her frown...

'Only when it's a lost cause.' His pager was bleeping incessantly now, and Hugh turned it off, impatiently reading the small screen with a frown. 'I was wrong. It looks like they *are* prepared to start the operation without me.'

'Then you'd better go.' Green eyes were looking at her, dark green eyes that weren't judging or patronising—the kind of eyes that might even make the canteen's hotpot palatable; the kind of eyes it would be so easy to open up to. It was the longest few seconds of her life.

'Go,' Rachael said again, jerking her face away, terrified he might somehow sense the sudden shift in tempo, hear the contradiction of her spoken word. Because surely her eyes must be saying otherwise?

Go was the last thing she wanted him to do.

A&E DRAMA

Blood pressure is high and pulses are racing in these fast-paced, dramatic stories from Mills & Boon® Medical Romance™. They'll move a mountain to save a life in an emergency, be they a crash team, ER doctors, fire, air and land rescue, or paramedics. There are lots of critical engagements amongst the high tensions and emotional passions in these exciting stories of lives and loves at risk!

A&E DRAMA

Hearts are racing!

THE SURGEON'S GIFT

BY
CAROL MARINELLI

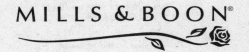

MILLS & BOON®

All the characters in this book have no existence outside the imagination of the author, and have no relation whatsoever to anyone bearing the same name or names. They are not even distantly inspired by any individual known or unknown to the author, and all the incidents are pure invention.

First published in Great Britain 2003
Harlequin Mills & Boon Limited,
Eton House, 18-24 Paradise Road, Richmond, Surrey TW9 1SR

© Carol Marinelli 2003

ISBN 0 263 83446 8

Set in Times Roman 10½ on 12 pt.
03-0503-44826

Printed and bound in Spain
by Litografia Rosés, S.A., Barcelona

CHAPTER ONE

AFTER today, it would only get easier.

Reminding herself for the umpteenth time, Rachael painted on a smile and took a deep breath before entering the office.

'Don't tell me you're the R. Holroyd rostered on for this afternoon?' The beaming face of Helen Wells was as familiar as it was welcome.

'The very same.' Rachael cleared her throat as she dropped her bag to the floor and rummaged on the desk for a handover sheet. 'Didn't Admin tell you I was starting back this afternoon?'

'When did Admin ever tell us anything? It just never clicked, what with the name change and everything. Had they said an R. Carlton was coming back we'd have splashed out on a cheesecake!' Jumping down off her desk, Helen crossed the room and embraced Rachael in a huge bear hug. 'It's so good to see you, Rachael.'

'It's good to see you, too,' Rachael answered truthfully. Helen Wells wasn't only an efficient charge nurse who ran the ward like clockwork, she was a kind woman who looked after her staff and was also a close friend.

Or would have been a close friend if only Rachael had let her.

'Are you on a late shift?'

Helen nodded. 'I'm doing a double shift, so I've been here all morning as well. We're as short staffed

5

as ever, so it's great to see you. But not just for that,' she added quickly. 'We've all missed you. How are you doing?'

Rachael glanced around the office, smiling at the unsure faces that greeted her. A couple of her colleagues smiled back briefly before pretending to examine their notes, others just downright stared. 'Fine,' she replied in a voice that was just a touch too loud and a touch too bright. 'Although I might revise my opinion once I've heard the night shift's handover. It looks as busy as ever out there.'

'It certainly is, and if Hugh here would stop tapping away on the computer and let me at the desk, we might be able to get started with handover.'

It was the first time Rachael had even noticed the doctor sitting at the desk, but she had been too busy concentrating on getting this first awkward greeting out of the way. Still, as he stood up, Rachael soon realised he wasn't the type of man that would usually go unnoticed, unless you lived in Sweden, of course. There, no doubt, six-foot-five blonds with green eyes and clear complexions were falling from the rafters, or yodelling their way down the mountains in droves, or whatever it was gorgeous Swedes did, but here in an inner-city Melbourne hospital they cut quite a dash.

Not, of course, that Rachael was remotely interested, it was a mere statement of fact.

Nothing else.

'Are you ladies waiting for me? I didn't realise.'

'No doubt you're only too used to keeping the ladies waiting,' Helen said in a teasing voice.

'I happen to treat the ladies very well,' he said with a slow smile in a deep, rich voice with not a trace of a Swedish accent, which discounted that theory. 'At least, I've never had any complaints.'

'Well, you wouldn't, would you?' Helen said matter-of-factly. 'One flash of that smile and you'd be forgiven anything. Hugh Connell here is our consultant plastic surgeon and resident heartthrob.'

Definitely nothing else, Rachael decided as she blushed slightly under his scrutiny. The tiny mole on her cheek took on gigantic proportions in her mind, and she automatically assumed that this dashing plastic surgeon was measuring her up for a new nose as he offered his hand.

'And this is Rachael Holroyd, formerly Carlton, one of our nursing sisters. Rachael's back with us after a year away.'

'Pleased to meet you,' Rachael smiled accepting his hand.

'Newly married?' His eyes were smiling, his question utterly merited, given the snippet of information Helen had so readily parted with, but the gentle pre-handover murmur that had filled the office stilled, the silence broken only by a couple of nervous coughs as Rachael stood there, wishing the ground would open up and swallow her whole.

'Newly divorced, actually.' In an attempt to sound casual her voice came out too loud, too joky, and as she took her hand away she noticed a flicker of embarrassment flash over Hugh's face as Rachael's own colour deepened. 'And loving every minute,' she added, but her attempt to inject some humour into the embarrassing exchange only served to increase the awkwardness.

It was Hugh that gave a slightly embarrassed cough this time. 'Glad to hear it,' he said, flashing a quick on-off smile which went nowhere near his eyes. With a brief nod he picked up his stethoscope and pager as Rachael sat down, her cheeks burning, trying and failing to focus on the handover sheet in front of her, aware she had made a total fool of herself.

Again.

It was an all too common occurrence these days, almost as if she didn't know how to react to people any more. Even the most basic of polite exchanges seemed to end in awkward blushes and not for the first time Rachael questioned the wisdom of coming back to work. If she couldn't deal with her colleagues, what chance would she have with the patients?

But sitting moping at home hadn't been getting her anywhere, and it certainly wasn't going to get the bills paid—there really hadn't been any other choice *but* to come back to work. Anyway, Rachael consoled herself, at least she wouldn't have to see that Hugh Connell much—after all, the surgical unit rarely had cosmetic patients. She was reading far too much into it. He'd probably forgotten the whole embarrassing exchange by now.

So what if she had made an idiot of herself?

At least she hadn't cried.

'The bad news is that all the beds are full,' Helen started. 'But the good news is that at least we can't accept any more patients. Oh, and, Rachael, I don't know if you're aware of it but we're no longer just a general surgical ward. We've got twelve cosmetic beds now or, as Hugh keeps reminding me, twelve 'plastics' beds, which doesn't quite have the same ring to it if you ask me.'

'Oh, no.' Rachael let out a groan as she ran her eye down her patient list. So much for avoiding Hugh!

'Oh, yes!' Helen said, but without any enthusiasm, completely misinterpreting Rachael's misgivings. 'I felt exactly the same.'

'So when did this happen?'

'Last month. The refurbishment of the private wing of the hospital is taking longer than expected so, rather than lose the admissions, they're being 'blended' into the public wards—and that's Admin's expression, not mine! The surgical wards were all supposed to take eight each, but because our ward's new and has the best facilities we've been lumbered with more than our share.'

'So they're private patients?'

Helen rolled her eyes. 'Private patients on a public ward—not the greatest mix at the best of times, and they're all constantly pushing their bells, asking for their water jugs to be moved two inches to the right. But what can you expect when they've got a doctor like Hugh?'

'What do you mean?'

'He treats them like china. Nothing, and I mean nothing, is too much trouble for him.'

'Well, he's being paid to be nice,' Rachael grumbled, but Helen shook her head.

'He's just nice, full stop, as well as a good doctor, which makes it hard to point out just how difficult it can be. He'd move the jug, so to speak, and move it again and again if it would keep his beloved patients happy. So a word of warning for you when you're in charge—it doesn't matter if it's midnight on New Year's eve, if one of Hugh's patients is unwell he wants to be informed. So whereas with most doctors you might sit on things for a while, don't even think about it with Hugh—he likes to keep his finger on the pulse.'

'He can keep it on mine.' Bev, one of the other nurses, laughed.

'And mine,' Trevor chimed in, which had everyone in stitches until Helen let out a yelp as she glanced at the clock. 'Come on, guys, let's get handover out of the way.'

Rachael knew that once the report was over she wasn't going to get away that lightly from Helen, and was already half expecting it when Helen called her back as she made her way out onto the ward.

'Here's your pager,' she said, handing Rachael the small fluorescent orange bleeper.

'What on earth is this for?'

'You've got Orange Bay.' She laughed at Rachael's bemused face. 'The new system is finally under way. Now, when a patient presses the call button, their allocated nurse is alerted directly by their pager.'

'You're serious, aren't you?' Rachael asked, slowly turning the small pager over.

'Oh, I'm serious all right. You can't escape for a moment, not even when you go the bathroom. And look at this.' She tapped the computer in front of her. 'This records how long it takes for you to answer the call bell—a bit ''Big Brother'' if you ask me, but you soon get used to it.'

'And here was me thinking I'd take up where I left off. A year's a long time in nursing these days.'

'It's a long time, full stop,' Helen said gently. 'We really have missed you, you know.'

'I know.'

'You're looking great.'

Rachael gave a thin laugh. 'You mean I've lost weight.'

'Not just that, you look fabulous.'

'Amazing what a year of stress will do,' Rachael said dryly. 'I'm sure Richard would still be able to find fault.' She tapped the edge of her cheekbone. 'I mean, look, horror of horrors, I've still got a mole.'

Helen rolled her eyes. 'So have a couple of super-models I can think of but, then, no doubt, that ex-husband of yours would find fault even with one of them.'

'Look, Helen, I'm sorry I didn't return your calls and letters...'

'You had enough on your mind.' Helen waved her hand dismissively. 'I'm just glad that you got them, glad that you knew I was thinking of you. So how are coping?'

'Getting there.' Rachael gave a small shrug. 'Helen, I know you mean well, and I don't want to come across rude, it's just that...'

'It's none of my business?'

'No,' Rachael answered quickly, somewhat taken aback at Helen's take on things. 'I just can't talk about it. I know talking is exactly what I'm supposed to be doing, but I just can't, especially not today. It's hard enough as it is, coming back to work, without bringing it all up.'

'Fair enough.' Helen looked at her shrewdly. 'But if you ever change your mind, you know that I'm here.'

Rachael nodded and turned to go, but Helen

hadn't quite finished. 'I suppose a girls' night with a bottle of wine and a pile of slushy films is out of the question, then?'

'With no secret agenda?' Rachael questioned. 'No waiting for me to open up and reveal all?'

Helen nodded. 'Scout's honour. I've missed you, Rachael, and our chats.'

There was twenty years' difference in age between the two women. Helen, happily overweight, blissfully married and successfully juggling four boys with her career, was a world away from a rather brittle Rachael who, as well as being far too thin, was newly single and having enough trouble juggling just getting up in the morning.

'I'll bring the videos, you can supply the wine. You did manage to get a couple of decent bottles from the divorce settlement, I hope?'

Rachael grinned. 'A couple Richard didn't know about.'

'I'll look forward to it, then.' Helen's tone changed, adopting a slightly more businesslike attitude she peered at her work sheet. Friends they might be, but at work Helen was definitely the boss.

'I've just given you beds one to four this afternoon. They're all pretty straightforward—two surgical, two cosmetic, all a couple of days post-op except for Sheila Cosgrove, who's awaiting her surgery, so hopefully you'll have a gentle start back.' As Rachael's pager sprang into life, Helen started to laugh. 'Famous last words. Hailey Watkins will run you ragged.'

However, it wasn't Hailey buzzing but Sheila Cosgrove, eighty years old and awaiting the removal of a large abdominal tumour. The delay in her op-

large part in her symptoms, exacerbating her pain and generally making things worse. Helping her with the spray, Rachael spoke in gentle tones. Although she had only just met her patient, Rachael noted with satisfaction how her comforting words seemed to be working as gradually Sheila's respiration rate and pulse settled to a more normal state.

'I don't like hospitals,' Sheila said, sinking back on her pillows.

'A lot of people don't. Is the pain easing now?'

Sheila nodded. 'A bit.' Her anxious eyes met Rachael's. 'Can you stay for a little while?'

'Of course. We'll give it a couple more moments and if it hasn't eased off some more we'll give you another spray and see about calling the doctor.' The chiming from her pager was unfamiliar and it took a couple of seconds to turn it off and read the message. Pulling back the curtains, Rachael saw that indeed there was a light above Hailey's bed. 'Is everything all right, Hailey?'

'I asked for some water. I thought you might have forgotten.'

Mustering as much tact as she could, Rachael smiled. 'I haven't forgotten, I'm just with someone right now. I'll get it just as soon as I can.'

'And you won't forget?'

How could I? Rachael was tempted to ask, but thought better of it. Her irritation was soon replaced by concern as she heard Sheila starting to retch. Reaching for a kidney dish, Rachael soothed the elderly lady, her concern growing as she felt the clammy skin beneath her touch. Pressing on the call bell three times, she connected the oxygen.

'Sheila, I'm just going to pop on some nasal prongs to give you some oxygen.'

'Everything all right?' Helen's face peered around the curtain.

'Chest pain,' Rachael said fiddling with the flowmeter. 'Could you page her doctor for me? I'm just going to run off an ECG.'

'Here…' Helen handed her a portable phone. 'We're high-tech now! You stay with her and page the doctor and I'll fetch the ECG machine.'

Thankfully the doctor came just as Rachael had finished the heart tracing. Though it showed no acute changes, Sheila's symptoms, coupled with her cardiac history, meant that she merited a full cardiac work-up and a dose of aspirin in case she was indeed having a heart attack. Through it all she clung to Rachael's hand as the doctor listened to her chest and took bloods for urgent levels, and by the time Rachael finally surfaced from her patient's bedside to check on her other patients a good forty-five minutes had passed. It was a rather martyred Hailey that greeted her first.

'Sorry, Hailey, I'll get your water now.'

'No need.' Rachael wasn't sure but she thought she detected a slight edge to Hugh's voice as he placed a water jug on Hailey's locker. He'd even iced it!

'I was just about to do that,' Rachael said quickly. 'I got caught up with—'

'It's no big deal. Hailey wanted some water, I fetched it for her.' Turning to his patient, he gave Hailey the benefit of a very nice smile. 'How are you feeling this afternoon?'

'I'm in a lot of pain actually.'

With a small frown Hugh checked her drug chart. 'You haven't had any analgesia for ages. Why on earth didn't you let the nursing staff know?'

'Well, they seemed so busy, I didn't like to make a fuss.'

'You're not making a fuss. If you have pain you need to let the staff know. Sister here will get you something for it straight away. Have you been doing your deep-breathing exercises?'

'It hurts,' Hailey moaned.

'But it's essential. I explained the importance of them before you had your operation. That's why you've got a chest infection now, because you're not doing your post-op exercises.' His eyes scanned the chart again. 'Her IV antibiotics were due at one, they haven't been signed for.'

'They haven't been given yet. I was just—'

'About to do it' Hugh finished for her. 'Well, could you see she gets them immediately, please?'

'Certainly.' Which unfortunately was far easier said than done. The new ward design meant that the drug cupboard no longer existed. It had been replaced by a drug room, which you could only enter by swiping your ID badge. The theory was that fewer mistakes were likely to be made with fewer distractions, the only trouble with that theory being that it meant two staff leaving the ward floor at any one time, and at precisely eight minutes past one there wasn't another free registered nurse available.

Hugh took the news well, at least sort of, even offering to check the drugs with her if it meant his patient didn't have to wait any longer. But his rather prolonged sigh and obvious irritation made it quite clear he considered Rachael disorganised, and unfairly so, when in truth she was an efficient and meticulous nurse.

As the door closed behind them the distractions of the ward might have disappeared momentarily but the designers had obviously never factored into their calculations the far bigger distraction of a blond giant in a bad mood, whose aftershave was practically asphyxiating her, his unmasked irritation making it hard to concentrate on the endless vials of drugs that greeted her.

'Sorry,' she muttered. 'I'm not sure of the layout.'

Luckily all the antibiotics were stored alphabetically and for the most part none of the drug names had changed in her absence, but the drumming of his very neat, very well manicured fingers on the bench only exacerbated her nervousness.

She showed him the vial of antibiotic and Hugh checked the name and expiry date with a brief nod. Rachael did the same with the vials of saline. Opening the controlled-drug drawer, she located the drug book before opening the box of pethidine.

'Seven,' she stated, showing Hugh the box.

'Fine. Where do I sign?'

'You're supposed to look before you sign,' Rachael said through gritted teeth. 'You're supposed to check that there are actually seven ampoules of pethidine remaining. The law requires it.'

'I did,' he said tartly. 'I'm not some two-year-old who has to use my fingers to count. Now, where do I sign?'

To add insult to injury, when it was Rachael's turn to add her signature, she realised she had left her pen at Sheila's bedside and no amount of rummaging through her pocket was going to produce one.

'Here,' he said with annoying calmness. 'You can use mine.'

'Thank you.'

'Do you have a problem with cosmetic patients Rachael?' Hugh's question wasn't exactly unexpected, given the chain of events, but it still hurt none the less.

'No, of course I don't,' she answered briskly, filling out the columns in the drug book.

'Well, you wouldn't be the first nurse on this ward if you did.'

'Then it's good that I don't.'

'You can see why I'm asking, can't you? Hailey had to ask three times for a simple jug of water, her antibiotics are late and she's also in considerable pain.'

'My other patient had chest pain. Surely you don't expect to leave a potentially life-threatening incident to replenish your patient's water jug? And as for her pain, Hailey never gave me any indication she was in distress—in fact, the only thing on her mind seemed to be the fact that she didn't have any water.' She was on a roll now and added her signature with a flurry as she continued. 'And if you'd give me a moment, I can draw up her antibiotics and they'll only be...' glancing at her watch, Rachael met his eyes with a defiant look '...fifteen minutes late, hardly a reportable incident by anyone's standards.' Despite her fiery response, tears were appallingly close now, and the very last thing Rachael wanted to do was break down—not here, not now and certainly not in front of Hugh.

'Look...' His voice was softer now and Rachael stared pointedly at the blur of her signature in the drug book as he spoke. 'Maybe I came on a bit strong. Of course, a patient with chest pain has to take precedence. I tend to jump in without looking sometimes, particularly in the last few weeks. Suffice it to say there's been a few teething problems with my patients on the general wards. Some of the nurses have the attitude that cosmetic patients are somehow less deserving of pain control, as if the fact they elected for the procedure should mean they're prepared to suffer the consequences. I know they can be demanding and difficult, but the simple truth is that most of them have saved hard or have waited a long time for these procedures. It isn't something they've taken lightly and they're scared of it all going wrong.

'Hailey doesn't ask for pain control because she thinks she'll get out of here more quickly without it. Unfortunately, in this instance it's worked the other way. She was in too much pain to mobilise and do her deep-breathing exercises and now she's going to be here for at least a week on IV antibiotics.'

He had a point, Rachael was honest enough to admit that. After all, more than a few eyes had rolled during handover when they'd discussed the cosmetic patients, but his unjust assumption had riled her and she certainly wasn't going to take the blame because a couple of her colleagues' haloes might need a polish. 'Well, that isn't my attitude,' Rachael said firmly. 'I've nothing against cosmetic patients and I resent the implication.' She could feel his eyes on her but still she didn't look around.

'In that case, I apologise.'

Rachael would have answered, would have accepted his apology, but the tightness in her throat and the tremor in her bottom lip as she battled not to cry made it safer to ignore him, the silence growing louder as he awaited her response.

'Fine,' he snapped eventually, and from the rather curt turn on his heel Rachael's inadvertent snub hadn't gone unnoticed. Following him out onto the ward, trying to keep up with his long angry strides, Rachael rued the day she'd decided to come back to nursing. One hour into her shift and already she'd made an enemy.

Well, Hugh Connell could go and jump!

What right did he have to judge her? What right did he have to make such assumptions and then expect her to meekly accept his apology? If his patient's drugs being ten minutes late was all he had to worry about, then Hugh Connell was a lucky man indeed!

He should try walking a mile in her shoes.

CHAPTER TWO

'SORRY it took so long, Hailey, it's just been a bit busy.' Despite her internal anger, Rachael managed an easy smile and chatted away to her patient. 'If I could just have your wrist, I can check your ID band.'

Everyone knew the patient was Hailey but policy decreed that two staff members check the ID band against the drug chart. Happy that everything was in order, Rachael expected Hugh to leave them to it, and was somewhat taken back when he hovered.

'I still have to check her wound,' he said by way of explanation as Rachael removed the cap on the IV bung.

'These have to be given over five minutes,' Rachael said, expecting Hugh, like most doctors, to take the opportunity to make a quick phone call or grab a coffee. But Hugh, Rachael was quickly learning, was absolutely unlike anyone she'd ever come across.

'I'm happy to wait,' he said easily. Which was pretty amazing in itself, but when he sat on the bed and started to idly flick through the newspaper and make small talk with Hailey, Rachael thought she had seen everything. Most consultants would have positively baulked at the idea of having to make five minutes of small talk with a patient. Hugh, though, seemed delighted at the opportunity and it was a credit to them both that Hailey couldn't even have imagined the rather curt exchange that had taken place only moments before.

'I was telling Rachael earlier that I remember her from the last time I was in here.'

'Was that when you had your appendix out?'

'Yep, Rachael here was just about to go off on maternity leave.'

She felt Hugh's eyes turn to her and she fiddled with the IV bung, trying to ignore the conversation that was unfolding.

'So what did you call her?' Hailey asked.

'That's the first.' Rachael didn't look up as she swapped over syringes. 'I'm just going to give you your second antibiotic now.'

'Your daughter,' Hailey insisted, pursuing the conversation despite Rachael's obvious reluctance. 'What did you call her?'

Glancing up briefly, Rachael saw them both look at her expectantly and knew there was no getting out of it. 'Amy,' Rachael said simply, turning her attention back to the IV, painfully aware that both Hugh and Hailey were waiting for her to elaborate.

'What a gorgeous name.' Hailey rested back on the pillows as the pethidine started to take effect. 'And I'll bet she's beautiful.'

'Very,' Rachael said softly.

'How long have you been back?'

She must have counted every tiny hair on the back of Hailey's hand but still Rachael's eyes didn't move. 'It's my first day.'

Hailey let out a small laugh. 'And here's us running you ragged. Your mind must be a million miles away, worrying about crèches and babysitters and the like. We'll have to treat you gently. So how old is Amy now? Must be coming up for a year.'

Slipping the cap back on the IV, Rachael patted her patient's hand. 'All finished now. The painkillers should start to kick in soon. If you need anything, just press the buzzer.'

Walking smartly to the treatment room, she tipped the empty ampoules and syringes into the sharps box. The footsteps she heard behind her were heavy and already familiar, and she could feel the animosity from Hugh as he banged about, laying up a dressing trolley.

'I can do her dressing for you.'

'It's fine. I just want to reinforce it.' He stared at her thoughtfully for a moment. 'You should add a postscript to your little platitude about pressing the buzzer, Sister.'

'Meaning?' Although Rachael knew where the conversation was leading, she was stalling for time, trying to avoid the inevitable.

'Meaning you should add "unless I'm tied up with one of my *real* patients" or "so long as you don't want a bit of friendly conversation".'

'I don't like talking about my personal life.'

'She was just being nice, for goodness' sake.'

'Look, Doctor, you might be happy to sit on the beds and tell the patients what you had for breakfast this morning. I don't work like that. I prefer to keep a professional distance.'

'So I've noticed.' He raked a hand through his hair and turned to go, but just as Rachael thought the lecture was over, Hugh had second thoughts.

'You're like a breath of fresh air, Rachael, you know that? You're a real charmer to work with.'

'I don't have to wear my heart on my sleeve to be a good nurse.' Rachael retorted.

'Maybe not,' Hugh said crisply, turning on his heel. 'But observing a few social pleasantries wouldn't go amiss either.'

As first days back went, it wasn't a exactly a howling success, but neither was it a total disaster, Rachael reflected as she sat at the nurses' station towards the end of her shift, writing up her patients' notes. It actually *was* good to be back. OK, the United Nations might need to draw up a peace treaty to keep her and Hugh from killing each other, but for the most part, the day had been all right.

Sheila had been reviewed by Cardiology and though her bloods and ECG had been reported unchanged, the event meant her operation had been set back further. Hailey, once the pethidine had kicked in, had slept for most of the afternoon, happily receiving visitors during the evening. And her other two patients had pretty much taken care of themselves, apart from needing some drugs and dressing changes. Everything Rachael had done during her shift had to be diligently recorded and as she sat there, chewing the end of her pen, she realised it was nice to be actually using her brain again, to be dwelling on other people's problems for once. OK, so there had been a few hiccoughs, but Rachael was determined not to dwell on them.

She had survived her first day back.

'They're ready for you.' Helen gave an encouraging smile as she came out of the office. Stepping in, Rachael felt a million miles away from the nervous wreck that had started the shift only hours earlier.

'Be gentle with me, guys.' She smiled before she started her handover. 'I haven't done it in ages.'

A few cat-calls showed that one thing that definitely hadn't changed was the below-the-belt humour of nurses, and with the help of an encouraging wink or two from a couple of old colleagues Rachael handed over her patients to the care of the night staff.

'They didn't eat you alive, then?' Helen asked as Rachael pulled out her hair tie and slipped on her jacket.

'They were fine. Everyone's been great.'

'So we'll see you back here tomorrow?'

Rachael nodded. 'Thanks, Helen.' As she went to go, her colleague called her back.

'Drop these into the doctors' office on the way past, would you? Hugh just buzzed for them.'

There was no getting out of it. Rachael hesitated before knocking. Hugh's blond head was turned from her as he tapped away on the computer. Opening the door, she slipped the papers on the desk. 'Helen said you needed these.'

Not waiting for an answer, she started to leave.

'Rachael, about this afternoon...'

'Let's not go there, huh?' She really didn't want to end the day on a confrontational note. All she wanted to do now was go home, peel off her uniform and slip into a warm bath. Rowing with Hugh again was way down on her list of priorities, but realising, in the name of patient of care, that something needed to be said if they were going to work effectively together, after only the slightest pause

Rachael swallowed her pride. 'I'm sorry for earlier. I think we got off to a bad start. Maybe we can start afresh tomorrow?'

The bitter pill of apologising was made sweeter by his quick response. 'I'd like that.' He had swung his chair around to face her now. 'I'm sorry as well. Some of my comments were uncalled-for. I'm sure I just got it all wrong. Helen's been singing your praises, and she's a pretty good judge of character.'

'I hope so, because she's been saying the same about you.'

Hugh laughed. 'So we're both perfect—is it any wonder we clashed? Anyway, I've held you up long enough. No doubt you're desperate to get back to your baby.'

Turning to go, her hand stayed on the doorhandle. She felt rather than heard him turn back to the computer and though she didn't want to do it, Rachael also knew that it was time. If they were going to have any chance of working together as a team, then some things were just best out in the open.

'Hugh…' The tapping on the keyboard stopped. 'I'm not saying this to make you feel awkward…' He swung back to face her, his eyebrows furrowing as he looked at her face.

'Whatever's wrong? I thought we'd decided to start afresh tomorrow, the rows forgotten.'

She nodded, biting hard on her lip, taking a moment to compose herself before she answered as Hugh watched her quizzically. 'I know that. Look, I didn't say anything to Hailey because she's only going to be here for the next couple of days so it didn't seem fair to upset her, but you and I are going to be working together a lot…'

'Rachael, I've no idea what you're talking about.'

'I know.' There was an awful silence...Hugh waiting for her explanation, Rachael wondering just how best to give it.

'I did have a little girl,' she started. 'Her name was Amy.' She watched as his quizzical look vanished, replaced instead by a look of cold shock, horror even, as he registered the past tense in her words. 'And, as I said to Hailey, she was beautiful.'

'Was?' Hugh's voice was more a croak, and he involuntarily winced as she nodded.

'She was stillborn.'

Strong hands were around her then, guiding her to a chair, gently pushing her down onto the solid seat behind her.

'Sorry.' Rachael spoke softly.

'Don't say sorry.' His voice was slightly breathless as he grappled to respond to her, the wind knocked out of his sails. 'It should be me saying sorry, Rachael. I had no idea.'

'Of course you didn't, no one ever does. You go off on maternity leave and everyone just assumes that you've had a wonderfully healthy baby and you're going to break into a spiel about sleepless nights and nappy rash.'

'But why didn't you just say something? I mean, Hailey was banging on about babysitters.' He winced as he recalled the conversation. 'It must have been agony for you.'

'It was.' Rachael let out a low laugh but they both knew it was void of any humour. 'Look, Hugh, how are you feeling now?'

'Me?' He stared at her, bemused.

'How do you feel now that I've told you?'

'Awful,' he admitted. Taking her hand, he gave it a squeeze. 'And really sad for you.'

'Imagine how Hailey would feel. Imagine how she'd have felt if I'd turned around and told her the truth. She only meant well, she was just being nice.'

'But you can't go around not telling people just so you don't hurt them,' Hugh argued. 'So that you don't make them feel awful. What about *your* pain, what about how *you* feel?'

'It was a one-off.' Rachael gave a shrug. His hand was still wrapped around hers and she fixed her eyes on them, not embarrassed at the contact, if anything, slightly comforted. 'Hopefully the next time a patient recognises me, if ever, I'll be a bit more…' she searched for the right word. 'A bit more…. Oh, I don't know, not so prone to bursting into hysterical tears perhaps.'

'Feel free.' Hugh's free hand delved into his suit, pulling out a heavy navy silk handkerchief, which he pressed into her hand. She stared at it for a moment or two, and then shook her head.

'I'll be all right.'

'I'm sure you will, but there's nothing wrong in crying.'

Again she shook her head. 'Accepting,' she gave a sniff. 'That's the word I meant. Next time I have to tell a patient, I'll be more accepting of the fact.' His eyes were on her his hand still holding hers as she prattled on. 'There are five stages of grief apparently, and acceptance is the final one.'

'Where are you now?' His voice was gentle, more an echo of her own thoughts really.

'Well, I'm past the denial stage, so I guess I've moved on to anger,' Rachael said with a trembling

voice. 'Maybe the textbooks do get it right sometimes, because angry just about sums me up at the
moment. I'm angry for me and I'm angry for Amy,
for all she's missed out on and all the pain I've been
through. It's nearly been a year now.' She nibbled
at her lower lip and fiddled with the handkerchief in
her hand as he still held her. 'That's a long time to
be angry.' Brown eyes, devoid of tears yet steeped
in pain, finally looked up, and she found herself staring back into his infinitely understanding ones. 'I
think I must be stuck at number two. Maybe I'm a
slow learner.'

'Maybe you've got a lot to be angry about?'

A tiny nod was all she could manage, coupled
with a loud blow into the handkerchief, the silk cool
against her face. It smelt of Hugh, smelt of expensive aftershave and extravagance, and it would have
been so easy to bury her face in it, to lay her head
on that expensively suited shoulder and give way to
the tears that were dangerously close. So very easy,
but so very scary. 'I'd better go.' Standing, she re-
trieved her bag from the floor.

'You'll be all right—driving home, I mean?'

'I'll be fine.' The brittle smile was back. She held
out the handkerchief then, realising she had used it,
hastily stuffed it into the pocket of her jacket. 'I'll
wash and return it.'

Hugh gave a tiny shrug. 'There's no need. I'll
survive without it.'

All of a sudden Rachael felt embarrassed, embarrassed and exposed. No doubt Hugh thought she was
used to this type of thing, used to baring her soul.

But she wasn't.

To date this was as close as she'd come. As close

as she had been to breaking down and exposing the depths of her grief.

'I'm so very sorry.'

Rachael gave a small shrug. 'Like I said, you weren't to know.'

He pulled her back as she went to leave, his hand finding hers again, and it felt so right she let it stay there for a moment as he spoke. 'I wasn't talking about this afternoon. I'm sorry for your loss, Rachael, I'm sorry to hear about Amy.'

Making her way down the long polished corridor, she walked faster, rummaging in her bag for her keys, unclipping her name badge—anything other than looking up and catching sight of the signs for the maternity unit.

Funny, hearing Hugh say Amy's name hadn't hurt. It had actually helped, helped make her baby more real, meant that she had existed after all.

Meant that there was a reason for the agony in her soul.

CHAPTER THREE

FOR the entire morning Hailey had been the model patient. Not once did her fingers stray to the buzzer and no matter how many times Rachael popped her head in or tried to strike up a conversation she was met with a polite smile and an assurance that everything was fine. Rachael had been allocated Purple Bay for the last couple of days but was now back in the orange bay. As she gently cleaned the fine wound around Hailey's breasts, the fact that her patient wouldn't meet her eyes had to be addressed.

'Hugh told you, didn't he?'

'Told me what?'

'Hailey?' Rachael's voice was soft but firm. 'I've had enough people unable to meet my eyes to last a lifetime. Dr Connell shouldn't have said anything.' There was an edge to Rachael's voice, which she fought quickly to control. Poor Hailey was already feeling bad enough without thinking she had caused unrest amongst the staff.

'I'm sure he didn't intend to, I just mentioned how nice it was to have the same nurse looking after me again, how hard it must be coming back to work and leaving your...' Her voice stilled for a moment. 'I guess Dr Connell knows me well enough to realise that I can't go five minutes without delving into someone's life.'

'You like a gossip, then?' They were chatting

more easily now as Rachael concentrated on doing the dressing.

'Don't we all? Anyway, when I spoke about you the next morning when Dr Connell did his ward round, he just said that I should go easy on you, that's all. He didn't break any confidences. It wasn't hard to put two and two together and now I feel just awful.'

'Well, there's no need,' Rachael said firmly, carefully strapping the dressing back in place. 'And you weren't being nosy or prying. It was a perfectly normal question to ask—in fact, it was nice that you remembered me. I'm just sorry you've been made to feel awkward when you were only trying to be friendly.'

'You should have just said, Rachael. You can't worry about upsetting other people all the time—you're the one who's living with it. It does get easier, you know.' Hailey's tone changed subtly, the slightly dizzy voice softened with a wistful note, and for the first time that morning the two women's eyes met, no longer a nurse and patient but two women who'd shared the same pain, the only difference being that one was further down the long lonely path. 'You do what it takes to get you through.' Looking down at the dressing that Rachael had just finished, a smile crept over Hailey face as she admired her new breasts. 'Maybe not quite as extreme as this but, hey, what the hell. They're just fabulous, aren't they? I can't wait to get them home!'

They were laughing so hard it took a moment to register that Hugh had joined them behind the curtains.

'Sorry to break up the party, ladies. I just wanted

to check everything was all right for your discharge home, Hailey, before I head off to Theatre.' Whipping out his stethoscope, he gave them both a curious smile. 'What's the joke? I could use a laugh this morning.'

Thankfully it was Hailey who answered. 'We were just admiring your handiwork, Dr Connell.'

Surprisingly, he blushed. Very surprisingly, Rachael found herself musing as she took a well-earned break halfway through the morning. After all, he must see more women's breasts than any man could wish for, yet a touch of female humour had made Hugh blush like a teenager. Still, that rather endearing trait in his character didn't go anywhere close to making up for the fact that she was angry with him.

Furious, in fact—for putting Hailey in such an awkward position and for assuming that he had the right to share what Rachael had told him—and when Hugh came to the ward next time she was going to tell him as much.

'Don't get up,' Helen said as she came into the staff room waving an admission slip. 'We've got a new patient coming in. I'm going to put him in the side ward of Orange Bay. You mightn't even get him on your shift, he's a direct transfer from Warragul so it all depends on the ambulances when he arrives.'

'What's wrong with him?' Taking the admission slip, Rachael ran her eyes down the scribbled note, her face screwing up as she read the rather graphic details. 'How can you amputate a bottom lip?'

'It's an industrial accident. It sounds awful,

doesn't it? Apparently the mid-third of his lower lip is completely gone.'

'Have they got the missing part?' Rachael asked. 'Will they be attempting to reattach it?'

Helen shook her head. 'It was irretrievable apparently. According to the doctors at Warragul it's a very neat injury though, and Hugh seems to think there'll be no problem repairing it. He's even talking about doing it under local anaesthetic.'

'Well, I hope he's as good as everyone keeps saying. This poor guy's only nineteen.'

'Oh, Hugh's good,' Helen said assuredly. 'I've only been working with him for a month or so, but some of the things I've seen can only be described as miraculous.' Lowering her rather ample bottom into the seat next to Rachael, Helen let out a rather too casual sigh. 'What were the fireworks about the other day?' When Rachael didn't immediately answer Helen carried on tentatively, 'I saw you both coming out of the drug room looking thunderous, and the atmosphere was hardly friendly for the rest of the shift. I put you in Purple Bay to give you both a chance to cool down, but this morning it wasn't possible.'

'You don't need to keep us apart,' Rachael said testily. 'We had a difference of opinion, that's all.'

'About what?'

'He thought I was incompetent. I begged to differ,' Rachael said airily. But realising Helen wasn't going to let things go that easily, she gave a small shrug. 'Everything I did on my first day back just made me look awful—the little crack about my divorce, being ten minutes late with my drugs...'

'That was my fault. I kept you talking after hand-over.'

'Normally it wouldn't have mattered, but Mrs Cosgrove had chest pain so I got held up. Anyway, they were only ten minutes late. Had it been any other doctor, they wouldn't have even noticed.'

'Hugh's a perfectionist,' Helen said knowingly.

'And as you and I both know, I don't seem to do very well with perfectionists.'

'Oh, come on, Rachael, you can hardly compare Hugh to Richard,' Helen argued. 'They're nothing alike. Richard was obsessed with your appearance, with furthering his career. All Hugh's interested in is the welfare of his patients.'

'You reckon?' Draining her cup, Rachael stood up. 'Hugh furthers his own career *because* of people like Richard, and if I'd listened to my ex-husband, no doubt I'd have paid a fairly significant portion off Hugh's sports car in medical fees. I'd say they were very much alike.'

Helen laughed at her cynicism. 'How do you even know Hugh's got a sports car?'

'Call it an educated guess. And, no doubt, in the passenger seat is a skinny blonde girlfriend with a cleavage to die for. He's exactly like Richard.'

'I think you're being a bit harsh.' Helen gave a cheeky grin. 'Hugh's much better-looking.'

'All the more reason to stay clear if you ask me. Anyway, you don't have to worry about keeping us apart any more. We both apologised and everything's fine.'

Until the next time I see him, Rachael thought wryly as she headed out to the ward, just in time to say goodbye to a rather gorgeous-looking Hailey, a new woman indeed now she wasn't in her night-dress.

'Look at you!' Rachael exclaimed with a smile.

'I feel as if I'm about to topple over.' Hailey giggled. 'They feel huge.' In truth they weren't huge. Rachael had looked at her patient's notes and had seen the 'before' pictures and despite her own reservations about cosmetic surgery, she could see why Hailey had opted for the enlargement. Hailey's before shots made Rachael look positively buxom for the first time in her life! Hugh's surgery certainly hadn't been drastic or over the top, anything but. Hailey was leaving the ward with a nice, feminine shape and a smile that would light up the whole of Melbourne. 'I bought these for the staff.' Hailey handed a large tin of chocolate to Rachael. 'To say thanks.'

'You didn't have to do that,' Rachael scolded as she took the tin and opened the small card attached. 'Thanks ever so much, Hailey, they won't last five minutes in this place. Now, have you got all your discharge medications and your outpatient's appointment?'

Hailey nodded. 'In my suitcase. Gary's just taking it down to the car.'

'Remember to do your deep-breathing exercises and to finish all your antibiotics.'

'As if I could forget. Dr Connell made his instructions very clear. I daren't get another chest infection, I don't think he'd forgive me.' She held up her hand and ticked off on her fingers. 'I've got to take all my meds, wear a support bra and avoid heavy lifting and vacuuming for the next month.'

'Maybe I should book in for one after all,' Rachael joked. 'I could use a month off housework.'

'You're fine as you are.' Hailey paused uncomfortably for a moment. 'I'm sorry if I hurt you—before, I mean.'

'You didn't, Hailey,' Rachael said gently. 'In fact, you probably did me a favour. It's better if people know, I can see that now.'

'It does get easier.'

Rachael took a deep breath. 'Promise?'

'I promise. Are you in a support group?'

'Hey, who's the nurse here? That's the sort of question I'm supposed to be asking you.'

But Hailey refused to be fobbed off and, fishing in her purse, she handed Rachael a card. 'Take all the help you can, Rachael. Who knows? I might see you at a coffee morning.'

Glancing down, Rachael looked at the card Hailey had given her. The name of the voluntary support group that had visited her in the hospital was familiar.

Painfully so.

For a moment Rachael was assailed with a host of images, so clear, so agonising that for a second the months rolled away, the year disappeared and she was back where it all had started.

Or, more pointedly, back where it all had ended. Lying in her hospital bed, her hands over her ears, trying to block out the lusty cries of the newborns in the nursery, her swollen breasts aching, engorged, a physical reminder of her desire to feed, to hold, to love.

Sue had been her name.

Sue, the woman who had sat on her bed, the

woman who had gently held her hand as she'd stared dry-eyed at the bland curtains. Sue, who had spoken eloquently, her quietly imparted words making some sense in the swirling fog of despair. Sue had given her a card then, the same card Hailey was handing her now, coupled with the same offer to keep in touch, the same gentle invitation to come along whenever she was ready…

'We'll see,' Rachael said as evenly as she could manage, and made a mental note to bin the card the second Hailey had gone, wishing this uncomfortable exchange was over. Hailey would have said more, Rachael was sure of it, but thankfully Hugh appeared to check on one of his patients and Hailey couldn't resist the chance to say goodbye to him just one more time. Unwrapping a chocolate, Rachael pulled out her file to sign off the discharge. She filled in her file, the page opening on Hailey's past history. 'Gravid 3, Para 2', which loosely translated to pregnancies three, live births two, the words written neatly, no indicator of the silent agony that so many, too many women endured.

With a sigh Rachael stood up, desperate for a moment's privacy, and headed for the IV cupboard, the one place on the ward that offered it. Hardly a cupboard, it was, in fact, a large room with rows of metal trolleys containing various flasks, the walls lined with IV poles and pumps, the perfect place to take five, to bite back the tears that seemed to be threatening more and more these days.

Damn Hugh Connell, she inwardly cursed as she blinked rapidly. Damn him for interfering. If he hadn't said anything she wouldn't be here now, hiding in an IV cupboard, struggling to keep it all together. Seeing him breeze past on his way back to Theatre, his wide shoulders obviously not carrying a care in the world, Rachael felt her threatening tears turn instead to anger. Stepping out into the carpeted corridor, her rubber soles didn't make a sound, but though she didn't raise her voice even a fraction, the sharpness of her words were enough to stop Hugh as he approached the lift.

'Dr Connell.'

'Rachael.' He smiled as she walked towards him, then turned his attention back to the lift, watching the numbers light up as it worked its way towards them. It was only then that Rachael realised he thought she was just saying hello, that Hugh thought she was waiting to catch the lift with him, and with a bit of a jolt she also realised that her unfriendly tone hadn't surprised him in the least.

'I was hoping to have a word.'

'What have I done now?' He gave a slight grimace. 'Or, rather, what haven't I done? I don't know where I'm at this morning. Helen just wiped the floor with me for not signing off on one of my drug orders.'

'Actually, it's not about a patient.' Rachael swallowed, her cheeks burning as he turned and looked at her more closely. 'Well, not directly anyway.'

'Oh.' She could hear the surprise in his voice but he held her stare. 'So what's the problem?'

'I'd rather not go into it here.' She watched a frown mar his perfect features but as the lift pinged and the doors slid open, all of a sudden the wave of courage, the explosive anger that had assailed her just moments before seemed to be vanishing at a rate of knots. 'It doesn't matter,' she said quickly.

'I'm sure it will keep. You'd better get back to Theatre. I'll catch you later.' Turning, Rachael walked off, furious with herself for not following through with her intentions, yet relieved all the same. She would tell him exactly what she thought, but later, when she had calmed down.

'You've got me intrigued now!' Rachael nearly jumped out of her skin as she realised he had followed her into the IV cupboard.

'I thought you were in a rush.'

'They can wait,' he said haughtily, but it was softened with a smile. 'They're hardly going to start the operation without me. So come on, Rachael, what's the problem?'

'You are actually.' And though she wasn't looking at him, though Rachael was concentrating on restacking an already neat row of IV flasks, she just knew the easy smile had vanished from his face. 'What on earth made you think you had the right to give a patient such personal information about me? Not only have you made things very awkward for me, you've made Hailey feel uncomfortable. She's spent the last three days avoiding me.'

'As opposed to you avoiding her,' Hugh said without a trace of contrition.

'What's that supposed to mean?'

'You're a great nurse, Rachael. You're professional, knowledgeable and you're also very friendly and personable—at least with patients,' Hugh added. 'And someone sitting in bed, recovering from an operation, hasn't much else to do but watch the staff. How do you think Hailey would have felt if she'd seen you being nice to all her fellow patients and then running a mile every time she tried to strike up a conversation with you?'

'I'd have handled it,' Rachael said through gritted teeth.

'By avoiding her,' Hugh said, unmoved by her obvious fury. 'The same way you handle your colleagues—running a mile every time someone tries to talk to you about anything that isn't a patient or a drug.'

'How dare you make such an assumption? You hardly even know me—'

But Hugh cut her off in mid-sentence. 'I *dare* to, because it is just that—an assumption. That's how we form our opinions of people. I've seen you sitting on your own in the canteen at lunchtime, I've noticed how you'd rather scald your tongue drinking boiling coffee in the staffroom than, heaven forbid, actually relax on your coffee-break and talk to your colleagues. From that, therefore, I *assume* you'd rather not get too close to your co-workers.'

'You're wrong,' Rachael flared, her mind racing for a crushing answer. But none was forthcoming and she had to settle for a second, but less emphatic, 'You're wrong.'

'Then have lunch with me.' He gave a small triumphant smile as Rachael practically jumped out of her skin. 'I've only two quick patients left on my theatre list, so I should be finished by midday. I can page you when I'm done and we can share a very questionable version of hotpot together in the canteen.'

'I hate hotpot.' It was a stupid response, pathetic actually, but it was the best Rachael could come up with at such short notice.

No notice at all, in fact. Hugh's invitation had caught her completely unawares. The hospital canteen mightn't be the most exotic of locations but, given her fragile state, he might just as well have been asking her to fly off to Fiji.

'Fine, then we'll throw caution to the winds and try the ham salad.'

'I can't. I've got things to do on my lunch-break. I have,' she insisted as he raised an eyebrow. 'My car's being repaired, I need to phone the garage and—'

'It's OK, I get the message, Rachael.' His pager was bleeping, Theatre was waiting—everyone wanted a piece of him, but still he stayed.

'I hope you do. I hope this will be first and last time you *try* to look out for me. I don't need your help, Hugh. I don't need anyone's help and I certainly don't need the patients knowing my business. It's hard enough as it is, without telling all. If that's going to be the case, I might just as well walk around with a ''fragile, handle with care'' label around my neck.'

'What would be so wrong with that?' Hugh asked. 'Why shouldn't you be treated a bit more gently, given all that you've been through?'

'I'd far rather be treated normally,' Rachael retorted, not quite with a snarl but with a definite curl at the edge of her top lip. 'For your information, I actually prefer it when people don't know what's happened. It's strangely refreshing to get through an entire conversation without people lowering their voices.' Clearing her throat, Rachael adopted a rather po face as Hugh stood there patiently digesting her outburst, listening as she lowered her tone and adopted the voice of a social worker. ''How are you, Rachael?'' No, that's not quite right,' she corrected herself. 'It's more like, ''How *are* you, Rachael'' or, and this one's my favourite, ''How are you *coping*, Rachael?''

'People are allowed to ask Rachael. They're just being nice, for heaven's sake.'

'Maybe.' Rachael shrugged. 'But I'll tell you this much, Hugh. Right now I'd settle for being treated like a normal human being.'

'Normal human beings eat,' Hugh ventured, his smiling demeanour such a contrast to Rachael's surly expression.

'You don't give up, do you?' A very reluctant smile was starting to soften her frown.

'Only when it's a lost cause.' His pager was bleeping incessantly now and Hugh turned it off impatiently and read the words on the small screen with a frown. 'I was wrong. It looks like they *are* prepared to start the operation without me.'

'Then you'd better go.' Green eyes were looking at her, dark green eyes that weren't judging or patronising, the kind of eyes that might even make the canteen's hotpot palatable, the kind of eyes it would be so easy to open up to.

It was the longest few seconds of her life.

'Go,' Rachael said again, jerking her face away, terrified he might somehow sense the sudden shift in tempo, hear the contradiction of her spoken word, because surely her eyes must be saying otherwise?

Going was the last thing she wanted him to do.

CHAPTER FOUR

KELVIN was very young, very distressed and, Rachael guessed as the paramedics helped him onto the bed, very scared. The nature of his injury meant that speech was difficult but he still more than managed to put his point across with the help of a pad and pen the staff at Warragul had thoughtfully provided.

'He wants a mirror,' Bill, the paramedic, said as Kelvin scribbled furiously and handed the note to Rachael with a shaking hand.

'Have you seen your injury yet, Kelvin?'

He nodded, writing rapidly as he did so.

'''Briefly, at the factory. It's bad, isn't it?''' Rachael reread the note out loud to be sure she'd got his question right. 'Kelvin, it's not for me to say. I haven't even seen it and I don't want to take the dressing down until Dr Connell gets here—he's the one who'll be able to asses the extent of your injury and what he can do for you. I'm going to do a set of obs on you and then I'll page Dr Connell and let him know that you're here.' The paramedics hovered as Rachael checked Kelvin's observations, following her outside once she had finished.

''Struth, I hope this Dr Connell of yours is good,' Bill said, scratching his head. 'I got a look at it over at Warragul when they were dressing it and it's a hell of a mess, poor kid.'

'He's not *my* Dr Connell.' Rachael grinned. 'But by all accounts he *is* very good.'

'He'll need to be.'

But as good as Hugh was reputed to be, there wasn't a lot he could do from Theatre. Rachael recited Kelvin's obs efficiently without small talk, realising he was in the middle of a procedure with the theatre nurse holding the telephone to his ear. 'He's in a lot of distress,' Rachael finished.

'I can imagine. They've loaded him with antibiotics already, but are you happy to give him a stat dose of 10 mg IM Valium? I'll write it up when I get there.'

'Sure, so long as you repeat the order to Helen.'

'Thanks. If that settles him enough I'll repair him up on the ward in the treatment room, otherwise the poor guy's going to have to wait until tomorrow. The theatres are full and they're not going to free up one for a lip repair.'

Rachael frowned into the telephone. 'I haven't seen it yet, but from the notes it's pretty extensive.'

'All the more reason to get it sorted. I don't want him lying there all night, imagining the worse. Anyway, it will take a while and I'd rather spare him a long general anaesthetic if I can help it. I'll know more when I get up there. Tell him I'll be about an hour, and make sure you get a coffee in now—it might be a long job.'

'I'm off at four,' Rachael said quickly, too quickly, the thought of spending a couple of hours with Hugh unsettling to say the least. Realising she had overreacted, she offered up an excuse. 'As I said, my car's being serviced and I have to be there to pick it up by five, so I really can't stay. One of the late staff will probably do it.' She was still frowning, still not quite convinced Hugh realised the severity of Kelvin's injury. 'I'll pass you on to Helen for the valium order.'

The poor theatre nurse's arm must have been in spasm with cramp because he nattered away to Helen for a couple of minutes, and whatever he was saying made her laugh.

'What's so funny?' Rachael frowned as Helen hung up.

'He just asked me to set up the treatment room.'

'Hilarious,' Rachael muttered as Helen swiped her card and let them into the drug room. There was a slight edge to her voice and even Rachael couldn't fathom why Helen's little tête-à-tête with Hugh had irked her so much.

'We were just having a joke. He asked me to give him a nurse with personality then corrected himself, said he must have thought for a moment that he was back in the private wing.'

'Ha, ha,' Rachael responded dryly as she checked the ampoule.

'You really don't like him, do you?'

'I don't have to like him,' Rachael pointed out. 'I just have to work with him.'

'Or maybe you do like him,' Helen said, pulling up the Valium then pretending to concentrate on flicking the air bubbles out of the syringe. 'Maybe that's what the problem is.'

'Where did you get that from?'

'Well, whatever your reaction has been, blasé certainly isn't how I'd describe it.'

Rachael gave an incredulous laugh. 'Believe me,

Helen, you're miles off the mark. Hugh Connell is the last person in the world I'd like.'

'But he's gorgeous. Any woman would give their right arm to court him.'

'This is the twenty-first century Helen.' Rachael grinned. 'People don't ''court'' any more, they date. And if I've been over the top where he's concerned, if you must know it's because he gets on my nerves.'

'Why?' Helen wailed. 'He's lovely.'

'He's opinionated, over-confident and he thinks he's God's gift to the medical profession.'

Tossing a couple of alcohol swabs into the kidney dish along with the medication, Helen gave a cynical snort. 'Whatever you say, Rachael. And for your information, I might be a bit past the dating game, but I'm not so out of touch I can't pick a honey when I see one, and Hugh Connell is just that.'

'Helen...' Rachael caught hold of her friend's arm as she went to leave. 'Stay out of it, I mean it. Maybe Hugh is the ''honey'' you say he is, and maybe, just maybe at a different place and time I might have even been the tiniest bit interested. But this is here and this is now, and I'm simply not. I'm up to here with men,' Rachael said emphatically, jabbing at her neck with her hand. 'And even if one day in the way distant future I surface from my self-imposed seclusion, good-looking plastic surgeons are way, way down on my list of the perfect man. I've been there and done that, remember.'

'So you're not interested in dating?'

'Not remotely.'

'Good.' Helen gave a cheeky grin. 'So can I put

you down for a night shift in a few weeks? It's a Saturday night so I can't get anyone.'

Rachael rolled her eyes. 'Anyone with a life, you mean.'

As Hugh pulled back the gauze, Rachael had to make an actual physical effort to keep her face impassive. The entire middle section of Kelvin's lower lip simply wasn't there any more. By contrast, Hugh seemed positively laid back, giving his patient an easy smile.

'Don't worry, Kelvin, you'll look fine. So fine, in fact, that I'm going to get Maurice here to take a few photos of you—he's a medical photographer. I'd like to get a few before and after shots for my scrapbook. You'll need some documentation, too, I would think. Is that all right with you?'

Nodding, Kelvin picked up his pad again. The writing wasn't quite so furious, thanks to the Valium, but, picking up his shakily written note, Rachael deciphered it for Hugh. '"How Fine?"'

'Good question.' Hugh smiled. 'It will take a bit of getting used to from your point of view because you're so familiar with your own face, but to someone who hasn't met you, apart from a small, fine scar it will be barely noticeable, if at all.' His clear eyes shifted from Kelvin and met Rachael's. 'Is the treatment room ready?'

Rachael nodded but her hesitancy didn't go unnoticed, and with the tiniest motion of his blond head Hugh gestured her to the corridor outside.

'Problem?'

Well he certainly didn't believe in wasting time with small talk. Taken back by the directness of his question, Rachael gave a dismissive smile. 'No, not at all.' Which wasn't strictly true, but Rachael knew her place. A professional she might be, but questioning a plastic surgeon as to his surgical technique was way out of her league. Hugh, though, seemed to invite debate and pushed further.

'You just seem a bit unsure about things. If you've got any doubts I'd rather hear them now and hopefully put your mind at ease. Kelvin's going to be looking to you for reassurance, and I'd like it to be genuine. Come on, Rachael, what's on your mind?'

'I just think we should be a bit more cautious in our optimism,' Rachael started carefully. 'I know I haven't done any plastics, but it's an horrific injury. I think "fine" is just a touch dismissive. Maybe it would be more prudent to explain things now.'

'And worry him unnecessarily?'

She waited for a few sharp, superior words, but Hugh's stance remained casual and his eyes carried on smiling. Although the confrontation was enough to account for her accelerated heart rate, Rachael couldn't for the life of her fathom why butterflies were fluttering in her rib cage as she awaited his response.

'Lips have an excellent vascular supply. They heal amazingly well and though you may not have done plastics I'm sure you've heard about collagen.' He waited for her to nod before continuing. 'That's just one of the options. When the swelling's gone down Kelvin and I will have a chat about the others. The scar will be very fine, barely noticeable, but he might opt to have a small tattoo to even out his lip line and if the lower lip is still markedly smaller, a more permanent solution might be to temporarily insert a small balloon which can be inflated gradually to stretch the skin. From there we can do a small tissue implant. So, you see, there are lots of options.'

Rachael gave a grudging nod. She believed him, but still found it hard to fathom that it could all be so simple.

'Shame you won't be there to see it. You might have a bit more faith in me then.'

'Promise not to shoot the bearer.' Helen was bearing down on them and, despite her foreboding introduction, she was smiling broadly. 'The garage just rang.'

'No doubt to tell me I need a new engine and while they're at it a new set of wheels wouldn't go amiss.'

'No, nothing like that.' Helen beamed. 'They had a rush job in so they had to put your car off until tomorrow.'

'Great,' Rachael wailed. 'How come they told you?'

Helen just shrugged. 'Well, they're hardly breaking patient confidence. I guess Geoff just figured he'd get less of an earful from me.'

'Who's Geoff?' Hugh enquired, apparently intrigued by the conversation.

'The mechanic,' both women answered simultaneously as Hugh listened intently, seemingly enjoying the brief gossip.

'Looks like you don't have to rush off now.'

Glancing down at her watch, an impish grin spread across Rachael's lips. 'Are you sure I've got enough personality for you, Dr Connell? I mean, I'd hate for you to be bored in there.'

'I guess I'll just have to put up with you.' His teasing tone made her grin widen. 'In the interests of patient care, of course.'

Helen only raised one quizzical eyebrow when Rachael went into the treatment room to check all the equipment. 'I thought you wanted one of the late staff to take over.'

'Well, it doesn't matter now that my car's tied up, and Kelvin is pretty anxious. It might be better if I stay with him, given that I admitted him.' Both eyebrows were near Helen's hairline now and Rachael busied herself opening suture packs and pouring antiseptic. 'Anyway, it will be interesting to see first hand if Dr Perfection is as good as he says he is.'

'Whatever you say, *Sister*. I'll just go and fetch your patient for you. By the way, Hugh takes size nine gloves, we had to order them in specially.' Nudging Rachael as she went past, she gave a saucy laugh. 'You know what they say about big hands…'

Big hands he might have, but they were as deft and nimble as a pianist's, and Rachael watched, fascinated, as Hugh set to work, his deep voice soothing as he talked to Kelvin, explaining his work yet sparing Kelvin the more graphic details. The radio playing in the background was a soothing, relaxing diversion.

The room was impossibly hot but it was a small price to pay for witnessing the predicted miracle. With magnifying glasses on and a light attached to his head like a miner's, anyone else would have looked ridiculous but Hugh, of course, wore it all well.

'You'll be able to enjoy a nice cold beer by the weekend, Kelvin,' Hugh quipped lightly as he worked on. 'Actually, better make it next week-end—you'll need a week of antibiotics.'

'He's asleep,' Rachael murmured as Kelvin's hand unclenched and his breathing deepened.

'I've bored the hell out of him.' Shifting on the stool, Hugh stretched his arms out and took a well-earned break for a couple of moments, and Rachael took the opportunity to change her mask and gloves. 'Hell, it's hot in here,' Hugh said, circling his neck to release the tension that had built up from concentrating for so long. 'Can you wipe my forehead?'

OK, so Rachael hadn't done Theatre in almost a decade, but she had assisted enough doctors and seen enough medical shows on television to know what to do, but as she lifted the small sterile towel used for this basic necessity she was overcome with a shy nervousness, Lifting the glasses slightly, she dabbed gently under the frames, swallowing hard before running the towel along his forehead. Even his eyebrows were perfect, Rachael thought reluctantly, dark blond and beautifully shaped. And despite the lateness of the day and the mask covering half his face, the familiar musky undertones of his aftershave still reached her.

'You wear too much aftershave.' The words were out before she'd realised it and, wishing she was still wearing a mask, Rachael struggled to combat the blush that was appearing, stunned by the words that had tumbled out of her mouth.

'I know,' Hugh replied easily, apparently not remotely bothered by her rather personal observation. 'It's just that I hate the smell of hospitals, all that antiseptic and Betadine.' He pulled a face behind his mask. 'Yuck. Though even I admit it's probably a bit over the top at the moment. I got a massive gift pack for Christmas, you know the type—matching deodorant, soap, body lotion, aftershave.'

And it would have cost a fortune—there was certainly nothing 'bargain basement' about him. Tying on her mask, Rachael tried not to think about Hugh at Christmas, exchanging presents, or more pointedly the undoubtedly beautiful woman who would have handed him that particular package. Instead, she tried to concentrate on handing swabs and dabbing the wound, but it was becoming increasingly difficult.

'Here comes the good part.' For the last hour or so he had been trimming edges, cutting and stitching, but as he removed the clips and pulled on a soluble suture, Rachael watched with undisguised admiration as the lip aligned, slotting together like a complicated jig saw until all that was left was a neat L-shaped wound. 'Just a few fine sutures and we'll be done.'

'That's amazing,' Rachael breathed. 'I can't believe how good it looks.' Kelvin was stirring and she moved quickly to reassure him, muttering words of comfort and reassurance as Hugh finished the delicate procedure. As the drapes were finally pulled back, the full scale of what Hugh had achieved only then really became apparent. The face that had been utterly, and to Rachael's belief, irretrievably impaired by this appalling injury was now restored, perhaps not completely, but way, way beyond what Rachael could ever have imagined. Kelvin, too, for that matter, because when Hugh handed his patient a mirror the tears that Kelvin openly wept were tears of relief and joy. 'I thought I was going to look…'

He was shaking his head in wonder, his eyes never moving from the mirror as he stared at the small L-shaped scar. 'I can't believe what you've done.'

'Don't get too excited,' Hugh said, pulling off his gloves. 'Tomorrow you'll look at it a bit more critically and you won't be quite so thrilled with me. Your jaw shape has changed and it will take a bit of getting used to, and there might be a bit of trouble with your speech for a while. Also, once the swelling goes down, your bottom lip's going to look smaller, but all those problems can be addressed, so remember that when you get a bit down.'

Kelvin nodded, offering a rather shaky hand to Hugh. 'Thanks, Doctor. You can't imagine what was going through my mind. I'm not a vain guy but...'

'You'd rather not walk around with a hole in your face.' Hugh grinned and shook Kelvin's hand. 'Fair enough.'

She had underestimated him, not just his surgical skills but his insight. Already he had anticipated the depression that would surely follow such a terrible accident and his foresight meant that Kelvin would trust his doctor, knowing that the obstacles he faced were normal and merited.

'How's it going?' Trevor popped his head around the door. 'Sorry—wrong room. I was looking for a Kelvin Adams, the facial injury.'

'That's Trevor's attempt at a joke,' Rachael explained as a rather groggy Kelvin finally put down the mirror. 'We've just finished. He looks great, doesn't he?'

'He does, and I've got a bedside full of anxious relatives who would love to admire Dr Connell's handiwork.'

'He's all yours.' Hugh wrote a few orders into the notes as Trevor and Rachael helped Kelvin into a wheelchair.

'You push off, Rachael, I'll take it from here.'

'Thanks, Trevor. I'll just get rid of the sharps.'

But Hugh had already beaten her to it, disposing of the needles and blades he had used. Many, less thoughtful doctors left that job for others.

'Thanks for that.'

'I think we've both seen enough of industrial accidents for one day, don't you?'

'I'm sorry if I sounded doubtful,' Rachael apologised. 'I honestly didn't believe it could be fixed so easily.'

'You call fifteen years of training easy?'

'I didn't mean that, I meant—'

'I know what you meant.' Hugh was smiling again, but though his smile was familiar the effect it was having on Rachael most certainly wasn't. 'So you admit there's more to me than just a pretty face.'

'"Pretty" isn't the word I'd use to describe you, Hugh.'

'I meant as a doctor.'

'Oh.' The newsreader's voice was droning in the background, warning of speed cameras and rush-hour traffic jams with the news headlines to follow.

'How about dinner?' When she didn't immediately answer, Hugh elaborated further. 'I promise I'll take you somewhere that hasn't even heard of hot-pot.'

Thankfully there was a lot of cleaning up to do and she could busy herself stripping the trolley instead of collapsing. She even managed a fairly even,

'It's only five o'clock,' as she tossed the linen into a skip. 'It's a bit early to eat.'

'Well, a drink first, then. It would be nice to unwind.'

'I don't come in unwound.' Turning, she saw that she had confused him. It wasn't hot in the room now, it was positively stifling, and from the slight lowering of her voice, the tiniest angle of her head, there was no mistaking the obvious—she was flirting. Such was the internal revelation, Rachael half expected the newsreader to announce it as the five o'clock headlines struck up in the background, but the newsreader carried right on talking about the dollar's performance and indices, whatever they were, and Hugh just stood there patiently awaiting her explanation.

'I only come in "highly strung".' Rachael said finally. 'Believe me, the unwound version wouldn't be very attractive.'

Hugh laughed, displaying very white, very even teeth, and as he peeled of his theatre gown and tucked in his shirt she caught a glimpse of a far too toned abdomen. 'I'm willing to risk it. Come on, Rachael, it would be nice.'

Nice.

What did men like Hugh Connell know about nice? Sure, they'd enjoy a meal, a bottle of wine, and maybe it would be so 'nice' they'd do it all over again at the weekend. But somewhere down the track, that wouldn't be enough. Somewhere in the not too distant future the gentle flirting would lead to bigger things, which meant laying yourself on the line, raising the odds of being hurt.

Again.

It was far easier to stop it all right here and now. To brush off his invitation with a smile and a joke.

'No, thanks, I think I'll stick with the highly strung version.'

He had loosened his tie for the procedure and now as he undid the length of silk and expertly knotted it again Rachael was suddenly assailed with a vision of him dressing in the morning, standing in the bedroom, getting ready for work. But rather more disturbing was her own guest appearance in the fantasy, lying on the bed, breathing in the seductive, heady smell that was so much Hugh, sharing a secret sexy smile as they silently recalled their love-making.

'I'm asking you to dinner, Rachael, nothing else.' His voice dragged her out of her fantasy but reality was just as dangerous. 'And if you're very good, I might even throw in a car ride home.'

As will-power went, Rachael had none, and anyway it would have looked pretty stupid to refuse such a casual offer. The only problem was, there was nothing very casual about her feelings at this moment. Nothing casual at all about the military band that had started stomping where her heart had been. 'A drink,' Rachael said firmly as the bagpipes made their debut, yet despite the crescendo of her internal nervousness, she kept her voice amazingly even. 'A quick drink, and don't worry about the lift—I'll take a taxi.'

But as his car remote blipped a few minutes later and the lights on his sleek black car winked invitingly, Rachael wondered for the hundredth time since she had agreed to go just what on earth it was she was doing.

The sports car was inevitable, Rachael decided, but the flat-chested brunette with a mole on her cheek didn't quite fit the picture she'd had in her mind.

CHAPTER FIVE

'WOULD you like to see the menu?'

Shaking her head, Rachael accepted her gin and tonic from the waiter.

'No, thanks, the drink's just fine.'

'I would.' With a nod of thanks Hugh accepted the card and with annoying nonchalance proceeded to read it, ignoring the indignant look Rachael was throwing at him.

'I said just a drink.'

'And I heard you. I'll take you home later, but nine nights out of ten I end up here anyway and tonight won't be any different. I'm just taking it out of the freezer so to speak.'

'Meaning?'

'I'm deciding what I'm having now and I'll come back to eat later.'

'Because I definitely don't want to eat,' Rachael reiterated.

'So you've already said.'

Another hefty sip of her drink killed about two seconds flat. 'I shouldn't have come out in my uniform. I look stupid.'

Hugh shrugged. 'You look like a businesswoman in a navy suit—it's not like you're wearing your name badge and stethoscope.' Leaning over he peered under the table as Rachael twitched uncomfortably. 'A woman in a suit who has terrible taste in shoes.'

'What's wrong with my shoes?'

'Nothing if you've got a thing about rubber soles.'

Why on earth had she agreed to this? Why wasn't she at home, watching television or ringing up her sister for a moan? What the hell was she doing, sitting in a five-star restaurant with this slick demigod?

The silence became interminable, for Rachael at least. Hugh didn't seem remotely fazed, shelling pistachio nuts and popping them into his mouth as he examined her with undisguised interest.

'So you come here a lot?' she said finally, just because she felt she had to at least say something.

'Yep. Have you been here before?'

Rachael rolled her eyes. 'Millions of times. It was one of my ex-husband's favourite places to bring clients.'

'And there I was, trying to impress you.' He started to laugh. 'Hell, I always manage to put my foot in it with you. So, what was he like?'

Rachael shifted in her chair, reaching for a handful of pistachios even though she hated the things. 'I really don't want to talk about it.'

'OK, you can hear about me.' He leant back in his chair. 'Single, no children, not even one traumatic childhood memory that I can blame a single thing on, no priors—'

'I'm sure there's been a few speeding tickets,' Rachael interrupted, grinning despite herself.

'More than a few,' he admitted. 'But I'm almost fully reformed. That's about it. I'm very boring really.'

'I doubt that.'

'Well, that about wraps me up. Come on, Rachael, at least tell me a bit about yourself.'

'I thought this was supposed to be a drink to unwind?'

He shrugged. 'I love a bit of venom. Come on, I promise I won't be shocked.'

'There's really not much more to tell.'

'Try me.'

Rachael tossed a mental coin. Hugh was nice, funny and, perhaps more to the point, the gin was loosening her tongue. And best of all, not once had he lowered his voice. Not once had he leant across the table with that meaningful expression and recited the fateful 'How are you coping, Rachael?' in the funeral director's voice that seemed to be reserved for her these days.

It was as refreshing as it was welcome.

'As I said, I used to come here a lot. The difference was, I wouldn't have been sitting in my work shoes. If I was on late shift I practically brought a suitcase with me—make-up, heated rollers, a camisole to put on under my suit. I bet if you looked in the boot of my car there'd still be a smart pair of stilettos. I could change from nurse to corporate wife in fifteen minutes flat, the queen of repair jobs. He liked me to look nice,' she added.

'You look nice now.' But Rachael shook her head.

'Nothing like how I used to. I had a permanent Saturday booking at the hairdresser's, nails that were almost a health hazard.' He looked on sympathetically as a bitter note crept into her voice. 'And the ability to chat to the most boring of clients and look as if I was interested.'

'Well, you've certainly lost that knack.' He laughed. 'You don't waste any time with social niceties now. How long were you together?'

'Eight years.'

He looked at her thoughtfully. 'That's a long time to stay with someone who doesn't make you happy.'

'He wasn't always like it. I was only twenty when we got married. Richard wasn't anything like that back then, but the higher he climbed up the corporate ladder the more he changed and the more he expected me to tow the line and support him, which in Richard's opinion meant constantly looking the part.'

'Which wasn't for you?'

Rachael shook her head. 'Look, I didn't want to slob around in leggings and a T-shirt, well, not all the time anyway. I just wanted us to meet somewhere in the middle. I loved dressing up at first, buying clothes without having to look at the price tag, getting my make-up professionally done. It just all wore a bit thin after a while. Sometimes I just wanted to stay home. I'd be exhausted after a shift, or upset about a patient—you know what it's like.'

Hugh nodded without comment.

'Richard just didn't understand. The truth was, he didn't even like me working. He thought it reflected badly on him, can you believe? His answer was always, "Give up, then." It was easier not to talk about it in the end, easier just to keep it all in.'

'He sounds a real charmer.'

'He wasn't all bad.' Why she was defending Richard, Rachael wasn't sure. Maybe eight years together deserved some loyalty.

But Hugh begged to differ. 'He sounds horrific.

What sort of man would leave his wife after she'd just lost a baby?' Her eyes finally met his, sparkling, defiant, but touchingly wary.

'Why do people always assume it was Richard who left me?'

'I just—' he started, but he wasn't going to get a chance to finish.

'Is it so unfeasible that women might want more, that we'd cling on by our manicured fingernails to a marriage that was going nowhere?'

'Of course not.'

'I left Richard,' she stated firmly. 'I left him three months after we lost our daughter and on the day that he signed me up for gym membership. The very same day that he brought home a brochure about Botox injections and having my mole "painlessly and skilfully" removed.' Rachael gave a cynical snort. 'Perhaps it was one of yours.'

'It was probably one of Dr Fielding's. In case you haven't noticed, I don't have to advertise.' He flashed a smile. 'My reputation precedes me.'

'Oh, you don't understand,' she said irritably, but Hugh wasn't about to be brushed aside.

'Don't you think I meet enough Richards in a day's work? Men who want their wives looking the part, women having surgery to please their partners?'

A deep breath gave her the courage to answer. They weren't at work now, and it wasn't a nurse questioning a doctor. 'But you operate on those women, Hugh, you make a living on women's insecurities.'

His face darkened, and Rachael wondered if she

hadn't gone just a bit to far as he leant across the table his voice low and curt. 'No, Rachael, I don't.'

'Look at Hailey,' Rachael argued. 'Try and tell me she wasn't doing it to please Gary.'

'She wasn't,' Richard stated simply, and as he saw the disbelieving look Rachael threw across the table he repeated it again more forcibly. '*She wasn't*. In fact, her husband tried to talk her out of it, but Hailey had it in her head that was what she wanted. For years apparently she'd sworn it was going to be her fortieth birthday present to herself, once the kids were all at school, she wanted to do something just for herself. Gary was beside himself with worry when she ended up staying in a week with a chest infection.'

'OK, then,' Rachael relented. 'Bad example. But surely most of your patients—?'

'What about Kelvin?' Hugh interrupted. 'Or burns victims or people who have gone through a windscreen and somehow lived to suffer the consequences? It's not all about vanity. I do charity work as well.'

Rachael gave another cynical snort. 'What, for housewives whose private health cover has run out?' Looking up, Rachael instantly regretted what had spilled from her mouth. She could see the hurt in his face, hear the horrible, brittle harshness of her words. Berating herself, she longed to take it back, longed for the days when the world hadn't hurt quite so much, when the good had outweighed the bad, for the days when she'd actually known how to treat a friend.

'You're out of line, Rachael.' There was an authoritarian tone to his voice, a tiny but intriguing glimpse of a man who most definitely wasn't a push-over, a man who was only too willing to stand up for what he believed. And for the first time Rachael realised that it wasn't just by some sort of fluke that she had ended up here with Hugh. This was a man who only went where he wanted to go, who didn't suffer fools gladly.

'I'm sorry,' she muttered.

His eyes narrowed thoughtfully. Leaning back on his seat, Hugh took a sip of wine and shelled a few nuts as she squirmed uncomfortably.

'I'm sorry,' she said again, a hollow laugh ringing across the table. 'I seem to have forgotten how to be polite.' And despite the sudden drop in temper-ature, despite the definite dive in ambience, she was grateful. Grateful for a man who stood his ground, someone who wasn't prepared to make allowances, to shrug and put her moods down to hormones, someone who was prepared to reel her in when she went too far. 'Tell me about your charity work.'

Hugh shook his head. 'Another time perhaps, when you're not just being "polite".'

'Please, Hugh, I am interested, honestly, and I am sorry.'

'Better not.' He gave her a smile that told her she was forgiven. 'It's one of those pet subjects of mine. If I start now, the waiters will be stacking the chairs on the tables and vacuuming around our feet by the time I've finished. I'm not going to apologise for my work, Rachael, I'm not going to defend what I do, but I will tell you this. If I even get a hint that my patient is in to please someone else, I refer them for counselling or simply refuse to do it.'

'Then surely they'd just go somewhere else?'

Suitably chastised, the argumentative tone had gone from Rachael's voice now, but her feelings on the subject remained equivocal.

'Not always. Look, I don't come cheap. Most of my patients are rich enough that they want the best.' He flashed that dangerous smile again and without a hint of modesty he carried on talking. 'I'm one of the best, and if I say no, sometimes that's enough. I say it nicely, massage their egos a bit, tell them that they're perfect as they are. Come on,' he insisted with a smile. 'Admit it, Rachael, you actually do have a hang-up with plastics patients.'

'I don't,' Rachael insisted. 'I'm a nurse. I'm there to look after people, not question their reasons for being there.'

'OK, then. But don't sit there and try to deny that you don't have a problem with the doctors who operate on them.'

Rachael shrugged. A grudging nod was all the answer he was going to get.

'Can I ask why?'

'I know you do great work,' Rachael started. 'I saw it with my own eyes today after all, but the cosmetic side of it, operating on people so they conform to society's "rules"...' She fiddled with her glass, aware she wasn't making the most eloquent argument, and also, despite her passionate feelings on the subject, surprisingly loath to criticise him again. 'It just all seems a touch narcissistic.'

'Possibly.' It was Hugh that shrugged now. 'But that's the world we live in, Rachael. Do you know why I went into plastics?'

'Oh, I can think of a few reasons.' Rachael picked

up his car keys and held them on one finger. 'Fast cars, good food, beautiful women.'

Hugh laughed loudly, completely unruffled. 'I'd have had all that anyway, without doing plastics.' He leant back in his chair again, rocking slightly as he did so, staring at her unashamedly. 'My playboy status is hereditary, I'm afraid. You'll have to guess again.'

'I can't.' Rachael answered irritated. So he had bags of money, loads of charm *and* he was a doctor to boot. Couldn't he at least have one small fault?

'Nobody dies.'

'Sorry?' For a second Rachael thought she must have misheard him.

'You're looking at a doctor who cried his eyes out all through medical school,' Hugh said in that snobby, gorgeous voice.

'Rubbish.'

'Maybe a slight exaggeration, but my student days and internship were like hell on earth for me. The lectures I could deal with, but you should have seen me on the wards.' He shook his head, half laughing at the memory. 'Most days I would have given it all up right there and then—in fact, if I'd had my way, I'd have been tossing burgers at the local burger bar now.'

'So how come you stuck it out?'

'My father had decided I was going to be a doctor from the moment of conception and there was no way he was going to let me give up that easily.'

'Didn't you want to do medicine?'

'Oh, yes,' Hugh answered with a definite nod. 'I was one of those kids with his nose permanently stuck in a book, or in the science lab—a real nerd, actually.'

'Don't try and go for the sympathy vote, Hugh,' Rachael said with a wry smile. 'No doubt you were the best-looking nerd in the school?'

'Possibly,' he conceded with a grin. 'But all those books, all those exams, all that work—none of it made up for hands-on experience, and my first day on the wards this old woman—Vera was her name—died, just like that, right in front of me. It completely freaked me out. I can't even begin to tell you how badly I reacted. If you ever hear someone passing on a story about a medical student with a face like chalk, knocking over water jugs on his way out of the ward, you'll know they're talking about me. It was a nightmare and I knew there and then I was in over my head.'

Rachael was laughing now, really laughing. He told such a great story, his features so animated she could almost see Hugh as a spotty nineteen-year-old student. 'And that was just the start of it. I was a nervous wreck by the time I'd finished my internship, avoiding anyone over ninety, begging mates to fill in for me...' He gave a small shudder. 'Then I discovered plastics—it was like discovering paradise. Right at the end of my rotation I landed in Theatre, completely by chance, with one of the best plastics consultants in the business.'

Rachael was intrigued now, her laughter fading as she saw the serious look on his face. Her gin down to the last inch, she leant closer, listening intently.

'You know how you felt when you saw Kelvin's lip come together?'

Rachael nodded.

'It was like that only a thousand times better. The mathematics behind it, working with the body, moulding what's already there…' He gave an apologetic smile. 'I could go on for hours here. What I guess it all comes down to is that I get to be the good guy, Rachael.'

'But some of your patients are sick,' Rachael said thoughtfully. 'Burns victims and the like.'

'Not by the time they get to me. Oh, sure, there's the odd one, but as a rule I specialise in cosmetic repairs. I come in at the end when they've been to hell and back and I get to do the good bit. It's a nice feeling.'

Her drink was finished now. Placing the glass on the table, she managed a watery smile. 'I'll ask the waiter to call a taxi.'

'Why? When I said *a* drink I didn't mean literally. I'm sure I can stretch to another.'

'Who's just being polite now?'

Hugh laughed as she sat there, rigid.

'What on earth gave you that idea?'

'As you've already pointed out, I can't be bothered with social niceties. I don't really know what you were expecting from tonight, but a fun drink and cosy chat just isn't me at the moment. I also know that I've been rude about your work so let's just call it a night.'

He stood up and though it was Rachael who was ending the evening the stab of disappointment that hit her took her back somewhat. She had expected him to at least put up a token protest. He came around to her chair and she went to stand, expecting him to move it out for her. Instead, he lowered his head, his deep voice so close she could feel his warm breath on her ear.

'The night's still young, Rachael. I'm going to the gents, and by the time I get back I expect you to have chosen what you want to eat.' His face was still there, his breath still doing the strangest things to her taut neck. 'OK?'

Without turning, she gave a simple nod. 'On one condition.'

'Name it.'

Her face moved, just a fraction but enough to view that delicious mouth so achingly close. 'Wash off some of that aftershave.'

A lazy smile, so subtle it was barely there, ghosted across his lips as he rose to his full height and left.

Sitting alone at the table, there wasn't much else to do *but* read the menu, and she realised as she licked her lips that tonight had been engineered by Hugh right down to the last detail. He knew that one glimpse at such a divine menu and she'd have no choice but to stay, and if Morton Bay risotto hadn't been on the menu she'd have definitely asked the waiter to call a taxi right there and then. Come to think of it, the mocha ice cream with bitter chocolate sauce might have been a deciding factor as well.

'Have you chosen?'

Green eyes were smiling at her, that gorgeous, huge yet beautifully proportioned body was lowering itself into the chair and Rachael gave in. The only person she was kidding here was herself. It could have been butter beans and Brussels sprouts on the menu and she'd have forced it down.

Hugh Connell was divine.

CHAPTER SIX

'DID he kiss you?'

'Helen!' Rachael said indignantly, kicking the office door closed. 'Stop going on about it.'

'About what?' Helen said innocently. 'Trevor saw you leaving together, and from the way you're blushing you didn't say goodbye at the car park.'

'We did, actually.' It was worth a try.

'So how come when Trevor looked out of the window you were climbing into his car?'

'He gave me a lift because my car was being serviced.' There was no way Helen was going to leave it there—she'd put Rachael on the rack if she had to. 'We just stopped for a drink.'

'And something to eat?'

'A quick dinner,' Rachael snapped. 'Happy now?'

'Did he kiss you?'

'No.'

'Come on, Rachael.'

Sinking into one of the chairs, Rachael pursed her lips. 'He honestly didn't.'

'But did you want him to?' Helen asked perceptively as Rachael picked at a stray piece of thread on her trousers.

'No,' she said, then slumped back dejectedly. 'But I wanted him to at least try. And if you ever tell a living soul even part of this conversation...'

Helen shook her head. 'I don't gossip.'

'Please.' The sarcasm was dripping off Rachael's tongue.

'I don't. It's because I'm fat and maternal-looking that people tell me the strangest things. I'd never pass them on, though.'

Rachael started to smiled but it died halfway. 'Why didn't he kiss me, Helen? We got on so well, admittedly after a bit of a shaky start, but by the time we'd had dinner and everything it was going wonderfully. I don't think I've ever laughed so much in my life, and it wasn't just me enjoying myself. I'm positive Hugh was having a nice time, positive there was something in the air.'

'Something like romance?'

Rachael gave a reluctant nod. 'I thought I'd at least get a small kiss goodnight.'

'Now, correct me if I'm wrong,' Helen started. 'Didn't you say that the last thing you want right now is a relationship?'

'I did,' Rachael sighed. 'And if this is the type of angst it's going to cause I can see why. Helen, everything tells me that I'm crazy to even be considering one.'

'Everything except your heart,' Helen said perceptively.

'There's a million and one reasons why I should run a mile. I've just come out of a bad marriage, just lost...' Rachael swallowed hard. 'He's a plastic surgeon, for heaven's sake! A plastic surgeon who drives a sports car and uses five-star restaurants like they're the local burger bar.'

'He's not Richard.' Helen put a comforting hand on her friend's shoulder. 'Is that where this is heading, Rachael? Is that's what's worrying you?'

'No!' Rachael shook her head vehemently then changed it to a reluctant nod midway. 'Possibly. I honestly don't know. Am I just setting myself up for another fall again?'

'He's not Richard.' Helen said again. 'And I'll tell you why in one little word—class. Hugh's got everything that Richard wants, but the big difference is that Hugh knows what to do with it.'

'It doesn't matter anyway,' Rachael muttered. 'He made it very clear romance wasn't on the agenda when he drove me home. Everything was going really well. He'd paid the bill, we went for a walk along the river…'

'Then what?'

'He just changed. We got in the car, and Hugh was just different all of a sudden. He was still nice and everything, still friendly.' Rachael gave a low laugh. 'That's the problem, actually. Suddenly that's all it was—friendly. Maybe it was just a drink after all, maybe I'm reading too much into it.'

'You've only known each other a few days,' Helen reasoned. 'Maybe he didn't want to rush things.'

'Perhaps,' Rachael agreed, but the doubt was evident in her voice. 'I can't explain this, Helen. I know it's only been a few days, and I can't believe I'm feeling like this.' She shook her head, bemused. 'I honestly can't believe it.'

'Hugh's not stupid.' Helen watched Rachael frown. 'After all, the fact he didn't kiss you made you realise that you actually wanted him to. Maybe he knows how burnt you've been and that you need to take things slowly.'

'Then again, he probably realised halfway

through the evening what a mistake he'd made in asking me out.'

'You're an idiot,' Helen said as the telephone rang, her tone changing back to the efficient ward sister as she chatted for a moment then hung up the receiver. 'Mrs Cosgrove's ready to come back from Theatre.' The friendly chat was over, the patients rightly taking precedence now. 'I wish she'd gone to a high-dependency bed post-operatively. If she'd had her operation tomorrow as scheduled there wouldn't have been a problem.'

'Dr Khan said if he waited until tomorrow it might have been too late. He's pretty sure that her new pain is caused by some gangrenous bowel.'

'Poor old dear. Well, if you need a hand just call, and make sure you don't bring her back from Theatre until she's stable.'

'OK.' Rachael stood up and as she opened her mouth Helen beat her to it.

'I won't say a word.'

Recovery was a busy place, and Rachael slipped in pretty much unnoticed.

'I'm here to collect Sheila Cosgrove.'

'Sorry.' Helga, the theatre nurse, didn't look up as she took Sheila's obs. 'I tried to ring the ward but you'd already left. Her blood pressure just dropped a fraction. I'm going to ask Dr Khan to review her again before we send her back. He shouldn't be long if you want to wait.'

'Sure.' Perching herself on a stool at the head of the bed, Rachael spoke gently to Sheila who was still very groggy from her anaesthetic. 'Sheila, it's Rachael, from the ward. We're going to take you back and get you into bed very soon. It's all done now.' A pale hand slipped out from the swaddle of blankets and Rachael held it, knowing how terrified Sheila had been in the days preceding her operation.

Rachael liked the recovery ward—in fact, she liked the whole theatre package. There was something almost hallowed about Theatre people wheeled in unconscious, healed and wheeled out again, the staff dressed in their blues with their ridiculous hats and clogs. It held a morbid fascination for her. Here mortal miracles really happened; here the surgeons played God and the staff watched with a reverent fascination.

And if Rachael hadn't fainted through her whole theatre rotation as a student, there was no doubt at all in her mind that this was where she would have specialised.

Another patient was being wheeled out now, and Rachael felt her heart rate quicken as Hugh followed the gurney. It was the only time in the short time they'd known each other that she had seen him out of a suit, and there was nothing disappointing about it. Blond chest hairs displayed above the baggy theatre blues, but even the extra-large, creased blues couldn't diminish the taut, refined lines of his body, the solid muscular thighs, the broad back. Peeling off his paper hat, he tossed it into the metal bucket. His blond hair was dark now, plastered to his head, his face lined with concern as he carefully observed his patient, his deep voice dictating his orders to the staff as he wrote up his op notes. Perhaps he felt his eyes on her, but suddenly their eyes met across the busy recovery room. Rachael managed a tentative, nervous smile, as he stared at her for a moment.

He did smile back.

Briefly.

His eyes did meet hers.

Guardedly.

'She's all yours.' Helga's voice seemed to be coming from a long way off. 'Her blood pressure's stable now. Are you happy to take her back to the ward?'

Checking the obs chart and her patient, Rachael hesitated. 'I thought Dr Khan was going to review her.'

'Her blood pressure's fine now. He can come and see her on the ward.'

But Rachael shook her head. She liked Helga and, perhaps more to the point, she hated confrontation, at least when it didn't involve Hugh, but Helen's warning was ringing in her ears and Sheila's welfare had to come first. 'I'd rather he reviewed her before I take her back.'

'Fair enough.' Helga's pretty face broke into a smile. 'It was worth a try. Do you mind sitting with her while I go and find him? I think he's grabbing a coffee between cases.'

'Sure.'

Rachael was positive that the only reason Hugh came over and spoke to her at that point was because he had to. She was convinced, in fact, that had there been another door to take him into Theatre without needing to pass her, Hugh would have used it. And the strained words that came out of his mouth when he briefly stopped at the end of the gurney only confirmed her doubts. The man talking in stilted fashion, addressing the top of her head, was nothing like the Hugh she had seen last night. Nothing at all.

'Having a busy morning?'

Rachael nodded. 'Not yet.' She gestured to Sheila. 'I'm sure all that's about to change, though. How about you?'

'Pretty full on.' He gave a brief nod. 'Better get back to it, then.'

Rachael mumbled a reply, managed a quick smile then turned back to her patient with cheeks burning, her mind whirring as she tried to fathom a reason for the change in him.

What had she done wrong?

Why was he acting so differently all of a sudden?

And though she listened closely to Dr Khan's instructions when he finally came and reviewed Sheila, though she chatted light-heartedly with the porters while carefully observing her patient every careful step of the way back to the ward, it was Hugh that saturated her mind. She knew then that she wasn't imagining things. Hugh had definitely been guarded, and not just this morning.

In the restaurant last night, just when she had relaxed, when she had finally opened up, when the conversation had flowed and her barriers had come down somewhat, she had felt him slipping away from her. When she had criticised his work, questioned his motives, been an appalling companion, she had held him in the palm of her hand. So why, then, when things had been going well, had Hugh backed off?

She would have kissed him.

If only he had tried.

'Is something wrong?' Helen stood at the head of her bed as Rachael checked Sheila's obs.

'No.' Rachael frowned slightly. 'At least, there doesn't seem to be.'

'So why are you doing her obs every ten minutes instead of half-hourly?' It wasn't a criticism and Rachael didn't take it as one.

'I'm not sure,' Rachael said thoughtfully. 'The operation went well, and apart from a small blood-pressure drop in Recovery her observations have been fine, it's just…'

'You're not happy?'

Rachael nodded.

'Why not page Dr Khan?'

'And tell him what? That I've got a bad feeling about this one? Hardly enough to make him stop mid-op and rush to the ward to review Sheila. He's been really good. He already reviewed her when I wasn't happy about bringing her back.' Rachael ran a worried hand across her forehead. 'Maybe I'm just overreacting. It's just that…' She stopped talking, her voice trailing off in mid-sentence.

'Just what?' Helen questioned gently.

'The last time I got a bad feeling…' Picking up a pen, she started to write on the chart but the slight tremor in her hand didn't go unnoticed by either woman.

'Amy?'

Rachael shook her head firmly and forced a smile. 'I'm being silly, comparing the two. I'll give the surgeons a page and ask them to come and review her as soon as they've finished in theatre. Till then I'll just keep a close eye on her.'

'They just rang—your next patient's ready to come back. Do you want me to send Trevor?'

Rachael nodded gratefully. 'I'd rather not leave Sheila.'

It was a tiny decision, but one that Rachael was very grateful for, grateful for the time to fuss over Sheila and make sure that the elderly woman was every bit as comfortable as possible. As Trevor arrived with her newest patient, so too did Dr Khan.

'I was just about to page you,' Rachael said as he made his way over.

'Why, what's the problem?'

'I just wanted you to review Mrs Cosgrove after your theatre list. I didn't realise you'd already finished.'

'I haven't,' Dr Khan said without elaborating. 'How are her obs?'

'Fine.'

He nodded briefly checking the chart and then gently pulling the blankets back and assessing the wound. 'Why did you want me to review her?'

Rachael gave a tiny shrug, wondering how to best voice her worries. 'I'm just concerned. I honestly can't give a solid reason. How come you came up between theatre cases?'

Dark eyes flicked up to hers and Dr Khan gave the same brief shrug. 'You will page me if you are concerned again.' His strong accent didn't mask the sentiment behind his words. He went to go and then turned. 'There doesn't always have to be a solid reason.'

Sheila surfaced momentarily, licking her pale lips. 'So thirsty,' she whispered, pulling at the oxygen mask.

'I know, darling.' Rachael spoke gently, her endearment genuine and comforting. 'But it's too early to have a drink. You've got a drip giving you lots of fluids, all I can do for now is moisten your mouth.' Dipping some swabs into water, she gently wiped the elderly lady's lips. 'Does that feel a bit better?'

Sheila nodded, resting her head back onto the pillow. 'How did it go?'

Rachael hesitated. Dr Khan had only written up the briefest operation notes. No doubt he would elaborate on his findings later, but for now there wasn't much Rachael could tell Sheila. 'It went well,' she said gently. 'Dr Khan's just been up to review you and he'll be back later.'

The pale hand again peeped out from under the blanket and Rachael held it. 'I'm glad you're here, dear, glad that it's you on this morning.'

'I'm here all day, Sheila. You just rest now, try and get some sleep.'

'Sorry to interrupt.' Hugh's voice caught her unawares and Rachael turned quickly, her hand still holding Sheila's. 'I spoke to Trevor, but he said that you were looking after Kathleen. She's had a skin graft on her left cheek, the donor site is on her left thigh—that's probably going to cause her more pain than the graft itself. I want the pressure bandages to stay in place for twenty-four hours. I'll take them off myself when I do the round tomorrow. If there's any ooze, just reinforce them. I don't want the graft disturbed.'

His words were formal, his eyes looking everywhere but at her.

'Fine,' Rachael said crisply, taking her cue from Hugh. If professional was how he wanted to be, then professional was what he'd get. 'I'll come and do her baseline obs.' Which she would have done, but almost imperceptibly she felt the grip of the hand she was holding slacken, just a fraction, again nothing solid.

'Hugh, pass me the sats machine.' He did so quickly, watching as Rachael clipped the probe onto Sheila's finger.

'Ninety per cent,' he relayed the findings.

Ninety per cent on its own wasn't a terrible reading but given the fact that Sheila was on one hundred per cent oxygen and only moments before her saturation had been much higher, it was a marked and somewhat ominous drop.

Rachael never missed a beat. In one movement she pushed the 'alert' bell above the bed and Helen appeared almost instantly. 'Page Dr Khan, tell him Sheila's saturations have dropped,' Rachael said quickly, blowing up the blood-pressure cuff around Sheila's arm and putting her stethoscope in her ears.

'What's her blood pressure?' Hugh asked, opening the intravenous cannula and pushing the flask of fluids through by squeezing his hands as Rachael lowered the head of the bed.

'I can't get it.' Her voice was clear but there was a definite tremor to it. Pulling her stethoscope from her ears, her fingers flew to Sheila's neck. 'Hugh, I've lost her pulse.'

But even as she laid Sheila flat, called her name and felt again for a pulse, Rachael knew it was over, that this was the beginning of the end for this lovely old lady. By the time Dr Khan arrived, breathless and worried, at the bedside, the cardiac arrest team was being paged.

Hugh stayed, expertly intubating Sheila with the

equipment on the cardiac arrest trolley before the anaesthetist had even made it the bedside. Rachael knew from what he had told her last night that he must have been nervous, but not a single water jug went flying. He dealt with the emergency in a calm, authoritative manner, only stepping back when the resuscitation team arrived. Helen stayed to help, re-laying the details efficiently to each and every doctor who pulled up breathless. Trevor pulled up the drugs as Rachael massaged the chest, only breathlessly stepping aside when the medics took over. They all played their part, all did their best.

Only it wasn't enough.

Amazing herself, Rachael somehow remained calm throughout. Her biggest fear in coming back to nursing was that she'd somehow let herself down, let the patients down, if she let her emotions get in the way of patient care. Even when the team had dispersed, when she was left alone with her patient to gently remove the equipment and offer a final prayer, still Rachael held it all together. It was al-most as if she was on autopilot, as if she couldn't quite bear to look at the bigger picture. But seeing the relatives, watching them say goodbye to their loved one, was almost more than she could bear. As the sharp sting of tears bit at Rachael's eyelids, the reality of the morning finally sank in, and it took every ounce of Rachael's professionalism to do her last act for Sheila.

Help her family to say goodbye.

Orange Bay was subdued. Kathleen slept on, blissfully unaware of the tragedy behind the drawn curtains, but the other two patients lay back on their pillows in respectful silence, nodding briefly when the porters arrived and Rachael pulled the curtains around their beds.

'I've paged Housekeeping,' Helen said in a matter-of-fact voice. 'They'll come to wash and make up the bed when they can—they're a bit snowed under.'

'I'll do it,' Rachael said in a slightly weary voice. 'It will be better for the patients in the bay. They've had enough to deal with this morning, without staring at her stripped bed.'

'No,' Helen said firmly. 'You'll go and have your lunch. It's already long overdue. How's your post-op patient?'

'Fine.'

'And how are you?'

'Fine,' Rachael said again, a touch too firmly. 'But you're right, I could certainly use a break. If Housekeeping don't come...'

'Then I'll make the bed up myself.' Helen shooed her off. 'Go and have something to eat.'

Hugh was in the staffroom, munching on a mountain of sandwiches, but for once Rachael couldn't have cared less, her mind too full of the morning's events to worry about last night. She nodded a polite greeting then sat down, peeling the foil off a carton of yoghurt, her mind a million miles away from the dashing blond surgeon only a couple of feet away.

'I've just spoken to Dr Khan,' he started, as Rachael stirred her yoghurt. 'Apparently there was secondary cancer everywhere—on her liver, her lungs. They only removed the tumour for palliative reasons, to give her some comfort. It was probably for the best.'

'Probably.'

'I heard you talking to her. She wasn't in any distress. If anything, she was just relieved the operation was over.'

Rachael nodded dismissively.

'Rachael?' Hugh's voice was questioning, probing. 'This must be really hard for you.'

'Why?' For the first time she looked at him.

'It's your first death since Amy.'

The directness of his observation took her aback. She was used to people swallowing nervously, going anywhere rather than there. 'You can hardly compare the two. Sheila was old, she'd had a life, she was ill…' All the platitudes that had stamped angrily through her mind were recited one by one, but even said out loud they offered not one shred of comfort. Yes, Sheila had been old, yes, she had been ill, but a beautiful life had ended, and the horrible inevitability of death had invaded once again.

'I didn't think it would hurt so much,' Rachael stated honestly. 'After what I've been through, I didn't think seeing it happen to a virtual stranger could affect me.'

'But it did?'

She nodded, but still the tears stayed well away.

'Is there someone you can talk to? Someone who can come over tonight, go over things with you? You shouldn't be alone.'

She waited, for what she wasn't quite sure—an offer, a suggestion of dinner?

'Perhaps your sister, Helen even…'

Staring down at her yoghurt, she could hear the concern in his voice, the genuine tinge of worry, but that didn't count for much, not in the scheme of things, anyway.

'I'm sure I can rustle someone up.'

'Good,' he said, standing up and picking up his empty coffee-mug. 'Someone ought to be there for you.'

Just not me.

He didn't say it exactly, but his omission didn't go unnoticed and Rachael knew there and then that she hadn't been imagining things. The distancing she had felt last night as he'd driven her home had been real.

Hugh didn't want to get involved, which she could understand.

Hugh wanted to stay out of it all, which would have been fine.

If only she hadn't already let him in.

CHAPTER SEVEN

IT WAS nice to be home, Rachael realised as she stepped out of the shower. OK, it wasn't the plush townhouse she had lived in for the last eight years and the furniture wasn't exactly showroom standard, but it was definitely a home. Nice, too, not to have Richard grumbling about how late she was, revving up the car in the drive, moaning she'd kept his clients waiting for dinner in some ludicrously expensive restaurant.

Nice not to have Richard, full stop.

Pulling on one of his ancient shirts that had long ago seen better years, she dragged a comb through her hair. Catching sight of herself in the mirror, she eyed her image for a moment, sucking in her cheeks, imagining the pout she was pulling with a quick burst of collagen. Then, craning her neck, Rachael parted her hair, quietly pleased to find that there wasn't a single strand of grey. After the year she'd had, Rachael had half expected to be a bottle brunette by now! OK, she wasn't perfect, far from it, but she was passable, pleasantly passable even.

Peering closer, she took a more critical look. Except for that mole, Rachael thought darkly. Richard might have been way out of line in the timing of things when he had suggested that Rachael have it removed, but she'd always hated it. Yes, supermodels had them, yes, gorgeous actresses painted them on, but they all had figures to die for, perfect, pert noses and huge eyes. Maybe it was time to do something about it. Her time with the plastics patients had been enlightening, to say the least, and a mole removal was the tiniest of operations. It would hardly even leave a scar. But it wasn't the thought of a scar that had put her off having it removed. Hugh had been right with his observations on the first day, though she'd never in a million years admit it to him, to anyone come to that. She *had* been a bit prejudiced, and not just against the doctors. Hailey's decision to go under the knife had just seemed so extreme, so… Making her way down the stairs, Rachael tried to find a word that eloquently described how she felt.

Superficial. That was the one.

But not now. Slowly Rachael was coming round to the fact that there wasn't anything wrong with trying to make the best of yourself, within reason, of course! The problems arose when you were so busy pleasing other people that somewhere along the way you forgot to please yourself.

Curling her lip around the beginning of a smile, Rachael pulled ice cream out of the freezer and collected a spoon on the way through to the lounge, reading the label on the tub as she did so.

'Five hundred kilojoules per fifty grammes,' she muttered, flicking on the television and settling back to watch exactly what took her fancy.

Richard would have had a fit.

It wasn't the most glamorous pose to be found in: a shabby old shirt barely skimming the top of her thighs and one hand clutching a bucket of double chocolate ice cream (with real chocolate chips). But when the doorbell rang Rachael immediately thought it was one of her neighbours come to tell her that they'd brought in the garbage bin for her or signed for a parcel on her behalf—certainly nothing earth-shattering.

Hugh Connell standing in the doorway was earth-shattering.

Disturbingly so.

'Hugh!'

'Rachael.'

'I wasn't expecting you—anyone, actually.'

'I thought you could maybe use a friend.' He held up an ice-cream tub. 'I remembered how much you liked coffee ice cream—looks like you beat me to it.'

With a laugh she pulled open the front door and gestured for him to come inside. 'Ah, but this is chocolate, and a girl can never have too much ice cream. Come in.'

'Or too many friends,' Hugh said, hesitating for a second before following her inside. The guarded look she had first noticed in Theatre was still there, but at least he was here and holding if not an olive branch then the next best thing. 'I just thought I'd see how you were doing tonight, after Sheila and everything.'

'I'm fine, Hugh.' When he didn't look convinced she repeated it, this time with a wide smile on her face as he followed her into the living room. 'Honestly, Hugh, I'm fine. I'm not so emotionally volatile that I'm going to collapse in a heap every time something sad happens at work. It was a bad morning, that's all, and nothing I can't deal with.'

'So you don't need ice cream?'

Rachael snatched it off the coffee-table. 'I always

need ice cream.' Aware all of a sudden that her attire was displaying rather too much leg and Hugh looked anything but comfortable, she padded out to the kitchen and popped the ice cream in the freezer. 'I'll just go upstairs and get changed,' she called over her shoulder. 'Have you eaten?'

Her question was left hanging in the air as she darted up the stairs and dressed at lightning speed. It was way too late to do a salvage job with make-up, given how Hugh had just found her, but it didn't stop her running a brush through her hair and putting on the subtlest slick of neutral lipstick. A pair of navy shorts was casual enough for an evening at home, but in honour of such a divine male in her house Rachael bypassed her jumble of T-shirts, set-tling instead on a sheer lilac top that showed a bit too much bra through its flimsy fabric but at least gave her a bit of shape.

'That's better.'

Her bare feet meant that Hugh didn't hear her coming. He didn't jump exactly when she found him in the kitchen, looking through the endless take-away menus stuck with magnets to her fridge, but he certainly seemed on edge. 'You haven't eaten, then?'

'No.' He looked up then looked away again, tak-ing great care to read the curry selection as Rachael questioned her motives for wearing a black bra un-der her very sheer top. 'Do you want to send out for something?'

'Sure.'

It was like sitting in the dentist's waiting room, waiting for the delivery. Worse, actually. Conver-sation was strained to say the least as they took it in turns to stand and hover by the window, as if somehow they could speed up the food by mental telepathy. For something to do, Rachael opened a bottle of wine and poured two glasses, which killed about two minutes flat.

'Hugh, you didn't have to come,' Rachael said finally when the ticking of the clock became deafening and she realised her hand was straying to a magazine. 'If I'd needed company, I'd have called my sister. I'm honestly OK.'

'I was just worried,' he admitted. 'And you didn't call your sister,' he pointed out.

'Because I'm fine.'

'I don't believe you,' Hugh said, obviously far from convinced with her acting. 'I saw how upset you looked during the resuscitation. I know that Sheila's death hit you hard. It upset me...'

'It's part of my job, Hugh,' she sighed. 'I can't afford to fall in a heap every time I lose a patient. Maybe I should come and work with you in plastics when the new ward opens.'

She had meant it as a joke, something to lighten the moment, but from the rather shocked look on Hugh's face Rachael knew he had misinterpreted her. 'I'm not going to stalk you,' she said irritably, 'if that's what's worrying you.'

He laughed, but it didn't quite reach his eyes. 'Of course you're not. Look, Rachael, we're friends...' His voice trailed off and it was Rachael that filled the distinctly uncomfortable silence that followed.

'I get the message, Hugh,' she said softly.

'What message?'

'Well, at every available opportunity tonight, plus a few others you've somehow managed to conjure up, you've been very careful to point out the fact that you're here just as a ''friend''.' She watched Hugh cringe as she carefully put the quotation marks around the offending word.

'Subtlety never was my strong point.'

'I worked that one out from your aftershave.' She was trying to be nice, trying to put on a brave face, yet all Rachael really wanted to do was cover her ears and hum loudly—anything to avoid what was coming next.

He forced a half-smile, did his best to look her in the eye. 'I just don't want you getting the wrong idea, thinking that I'm after something else.'

'I don't,' she said firmly.

'I like you, Rachael, it's just—'

'Just not in that way.' Rachael finished the sentence for him as the doorbell rang loudly, pathetically pleased at the diversion the arrival of the curry gave them both, all too aware she was blushing furiously. 'Would it help if I told you that I feel exactly the same?' she added lightly, half expecting her nose to spout another couple of inches as she lied through her teeth, pointedly ignoring the fifty-dollar note Hugh was holding out to her as Rachael rummaged through her purse. 'The very last thing I need right now is a relationship.' She took the note with an apologetic shrug. 'You'll have to pay after all. I haven't had a chance to go the cash machine. I'll get it next time, *friend*.' She gave a cheeky wink as she took the money.

'So you're fine with it?'

'Absolutely. I've got lots of male friends.' She tried to think of an example but the only male that popped into mind was Trevor and, given where his sexual preferences lay, Rachael wasn't too sure that Trevor counted for much. 'There's no reason that men and women can't be friends,' Rachael called over her shoulder as she pulled open the door. 'Everyone says so.'

Rubbish.

Absolute rubbish.

Whoever had come up with that little gem deserved to be taken out and shot at dawn, Rachael thought angrily as she paid Rajid and banged about in the kitchen, finding cutlery and plates.

Whoever had said that obviously didn't have to put up with the Hugh Connells of the world. They should have, at the very least, put in an exclusion clause for men like Hugh. How could you possibly be 'friends' with someone who quite simply oozed sexuality? How could an evening with someone as divine as Hugh possibly be described as pleasant if it didn't end up in bed?

Bed!

Taking a huge slug of wine as she knelt down at the table, Rachael acknowledged, perhaps for the first time since she had met him, that bed was exactly what she wanted from Hugh—bed and then breakfast, lunch and dinner, and hopefully bed all over again. But it wasn't just bed that she wanted him for. She wanted him for all the other bits in between as well—the laughs, the tears, the 'Honey, I'm home', no matter how corny it sounded. She wanted to see him smile. Not the doctor smile, not the friendly smile he imparted so readily, but the Hugh smile, the one that held her entranced, the private, exclusive one Rachael was convinced she had seen at the restaurant.

She wanted to be there when he put on his after-shave in the morning.

Wanted to be there when he showered it off at night.

Rachael wanted the lot.

But Hugh, for whatever reason, had decided against taking things further. In fact, he wanted to do a rewind. To take out all the tension that had crackled in the air since the day they had met, to somehow erase all the gentle flirting and heady little undertones that had been so much a part of them, and revert instead to a pat-on-the-back, share-a-joke-and-a-laugh type of thing.

Perhaps she could do it, Rachael mused. Maybe a couple of months from now they'd be ringing each other up and panicking about what to wear for their hot dates that weekend, or gossiping long and hard into the night about the subplot of *ER* and the terrible food in the hospital canteen.

Fat chance, Rachael thought, tearing her naan bread and smiling at Hugh across the table, her face not for a second betraying the jumble of thoughts racing through her mind.

But it was friends or nothing.

And nothing of Hugh was more than Rachael could deal with right now.

'How about the movies at the weekend?' She saw the tiniest frown on his brow. 'If something better comes up, and by that I mean a very hot date, you're allowed to cancel.' She popped the bread into her mouth. And because Hugh was out of bounds, because that sort of thing wasn't supposed to matter any more, Rachael didn't bother to stop talking. 'Friends understand that sort of thing.'

'Sounds great,' Hugh said with almost as much reluctance as Rachael felt.

But great it wasn't.

Friends shared their popcorn and sweets without having to ask, friends didn't jump a mile if their knees touched or their elbows clashed when they sat down, and friends didn't have to apologise when the movie turned out to be the worst possible choice of films, given what Rachael had been through.

'Sorry.' Hugh grimaced, finally turning to face her. 'I didn't realise it was going to be a weepy.'

'Doesn't matter.' Popping a sweet into her mouth, Rachael tried to pay attention to the faces on the screen, tried to work up some interest in the movie, but it might just as well have been in Japanese for all the attention she was paying it, her mind utterly sidetracked, her skin so aware of who sat just inches away. She felt like a gauche teenager, waiting for him to cough and slip his arm around her or for his hand to work its way over and 'accidentally' end up in hers.

But it didn't. Not even when some of the audience broke into noisy sobs did he as much as press a handkerchief into her hand.

'The newspaper never said that it was so tragic.' Hugh turned, his eyes looking distinctly glassy. 'How come you're not crying? I thought girls were supposed to break up at this sort of thing.'

'It's just a movie,' Rachael said out of the corner of her mouth, wondering how someone as large as Hugh could shrink so far back into his seat just to avoid touching her. 'And I'm hardly a girl.' Turning, she faced him, trying to read his face in the darkness, occasionally illuminated by the flickering screen. 'I'm a woman, actually.' He turned back to the film, grabbing a handful of popcorn as he did so, totally immersed in the film, not listening as Rachael slid down in her seat, muttering furiously under her breath, 'Just in case you haven't noticed.'

'But why does he just want to be friends?'

They were sitting in Rachael's living room, face masks cracking, their toes separated by wads of cotton wool, diligently pushing back cuticles.

It was nice to have Helen back in her life, nice to be having a girls' night in after so long.

'I don't know, he obviously just doesn't fancy me,' Rachael answered, trying not to move her lips too much. 'Men and women can be friends,' Rachel went on as authoritatively as she could with a face full of clay. 'There's far more to a relationship than just sex. Can I wash this mask off yet?'

'Not for another ten minutes.' Handing Rachael a bottle of red nail varnish, Helen's face mask crumpled under the strain as she started to laugh. 'Just who are you trying to kid, Rachael? Hugh and *I* are friends, good friends at that, and I'm telling you now, the way he looks at me doesn't compare to the way he looks at you. Of course he fancies you, he's crazy about you.'

'Well, he doesn't act it,' Rachael sighed. 'We've done the movies, the casual meals, he's even been shopping with me and it always ends up the same way—an awkward goodbye and a whole heap of frustration. We're not even that good at being friends really, we're either arguing or apologising half the time, and I can hardly imagine him sitting here now, watching me in a face mask and choosing between Racy Red nail varnish or Classic Coral. Maybe he's gay!' Rachael added hopefully. 'Maybe that's why he's not interested.'

'Hugh Connell's definitely not gay,' Helen said in an assured voice. 'You might think I'm past it, but I can tell a hot-blooded male when I see one. Anyway, he briefly dated Helga in Theatre.'

'Helga?'

'The pretty little blonde one,' Helen said, absolutely unnecessarily. 'I think she's from Scandinavia or something—at least, she's got an accent and those gorgeous Nordic looks.'

'I get the picture,' Rachael snapped.

'You need to seduce him.'

'I think I've humiliated myself enough where Hugh Connell's concerned, don't you?' Rachael retorted smartly. But Helen's words had hit a nerve. In fact, seducing Hugh was something she'd actually thought about, to find out once and for all if all the sexual awareness, which she was so sure was present that she could almost taste it, really was, in fact, just a product of her imagination. And if it wasn't, if Hugh's feelings for her were far more then he was admitting to, then it was time to find out. Despite her surly answer, despite pretending to concentrate on her toenails, she held her breath, hoping that Helen would elaborate.

And in a style that was so much Helen, Rachael didn't have to wait for long. 'The trick is not to let him think you're trying so if nothing comes of it, if it doesn't work, then you'll have lost nothing.'

'Except my self-pride,' Rachael muttered.

'He'll have no idea,' Helen insisted. 'You can use my old going-to-the-beach trick. It worked on my

Jack, that's how I got him to finally admit he was crazy about me. Take it from me, it's foolproof.'

'But is it Hugh-proof?' Ten minutes were up, she had every reason to get up and wash the mask off, every reason to end this ridiculous conversation right here and now, but desperate times called for desperate measures and by the time Helen had told her down to the last detail how to find out once and for all just how Hugh felt, their face packs had practically evaporated.

'The manufacturer lied, I've still got lines,' Helen said dispiritedly as she came back into the living room a few minutes later, patting her face with a bath towel. 'What are you grinning about?'

'I'm going to make a call.' Rachael laughed as Helen gave a whoop of delight. 'The news just said it's going to be in the high thirties tomorrow, just the weather for a day at the beach with a friend.'

For once the weather report was right. Beach day dawned with not a cloud in the sky, the air was hot and sultry, just the sort of day you could get burnt if you weren't *very* careful. A vast picnic basket took up most of her tiny hallway and when Hugh arrived, bang on time as usual, Rachael had to be careful not to trip over it as she answered the door.

'You're early.' She grinned.

'You said ten.'

'Did I? I thought I said ten-thirty. It doesn't matter,' Rachael lied easily. 'Come in, I'm nearly ready.'

Dressed in nothing but a tiny red bikini, she should have felt awkward, but amazingly she didn't, she felt empowered, in control. Today she was finally going to find out just what Hugh felt for her. Find out once and for all if the attraction she felt was mutual.

'What's in the basket?' Hugh was taking a great interest in the wicker basket as Rachael made her way into the lounge.

'Oh, just some chicken pieces, cheese and wine, that sort of thing. Did you bring a towel?'

'Yep, it's in the car. I'll go and load this while you, er...' he gave a small cough as he bent to pick up the basket '...get dressed.'

'Leave the basket,' Rachael yelped, dragging him, despite his reluctance, into the living room. 'Sit down for ten minutes, I shan't be long.'

Hugh sat, it wasn't as if he had much choice. And as Rachael reached for the sunscreen strategically, but very casually placed on the coffee-table, Hugh picked up the remote and flicked on the television.

'It might even hit forty degrees today,' Rachael said casually, popping open the lid and squeezing a generous dollop in to her hands then offering him the tube. 'You'd better put some sun block on.'

'I already did,' Hugh replied not bothering to look up. 'Back home.'

She oiled her arms, her face, her calves as he sat unmoved, staring at a football show. It might just as well have been Helen sitting there, watching television, for all the impact Rachael was having. Lifting her leg, she placed her foot on the coffee-table, squeezing the tube directly this time onto her thigh and working the cream into her legs in slow circular motions as Hugh furiously worked the remote.

'The cricket's just starting, I really wanted to see this.'

Resisting the urge to hurl the bottle of sunscreen at the television, Rachael instead handed it to Hugh. 'Do you mind doing my back? I always end up missing a bit.' Turning, she lifted her hair, moving the shoestring strap of her bikini just an inch sideways.

'Don't you think it's a bit hot for the beach?'
She could feel his warm breath on her shoulder, hear him squeezing the liquid into his palm, and she waited, waited for his fingers on her back, waited for him to suggest they give the beach a miss and head upstairs instead.

'Maybe,' she whispered, her voice expectant, her skin tingling in anticipation.

'I could nip out to the bottle shop and get some beers. We could watch the cricket and ring out for pizza.'

'Ring for pizza?' She swung round, much too fast for someone in such a small bikini, and had to deal with the indignity of an escaping right breast as he stood there, staring fixedly at the television then thumping a fist in the air as one of the Aussies took a particularly spectacular catch. 'I hate pizza.'

'Chinese, then.' Hugh shrugged. 'Or we could get Indian again.'

'But I hate cricket.'

For the first time that morning their eyes met, brown on green. Defiant eyes, with not a trace of friendliness between them.

'And I'm not in the mood for the beach.'

'Well, I am,' Rachael retorted. She felt stupid, embarrassed and rejected all at once, and suddenly

the red bikini didn't feel remotely sexy any more—
she might just as well have been wearing a garbage
bag. Pulling on her shorts and T-shirt, she slipped
her feet into a pair of thongs. 'And if you don't want
to come then I'll go by myself.'

'Fine,' he answered smartly, picking up his keys.

'Fine,' she bit back, watching him stalk out of her
lounge and into the hall.

It was the longest, most humiliating walk of her
life, and she'd only got as far as the front door. He
didn't want her, he'd spelt it out, told her in no
uncertain terms that friends was as far as they were
ever going to go, yet Rachael had chosen not to
listen.

And now she was suffering the consequences.

'Do you need a hand with the basket?'

She shook her head, picking up the beastly thing
herself and marching proudly out to her car as he
headed for his own.

'I'll see you at work tomorrow,' Hugh called over
his shoulder, not even bothering to look back.

'If you can tear yourself away from the cricket.'

CHAPTER EIGHT

'TAKE Rachael,' Helen said brightly as Rachael deposited a pile of files on the nurses' station.

'Take me where?' Rachael replied absentmindedly, her mind focussed elsewhere, utterly determined not to notice how gorgeous Hugh looked this morning, fresh from his post-op shower, writing his notes at the bench, that ridiculous aftershave wafting over the desk between them. It had been two weeks since her attempted seduction, two weeks of burning with humiliation as she remembered every ghastly detail. Two weeks of Hugh deliberately ignoring her or when he absolutely had to, when protocol allowed for nothing else, referring to her as 'Sister' and speaking very abruptly.

'To the fundraising ball on Saturday.' Ignoring Rachael's frantic eyes signals, Helen carried on happily, 'The plastics unit is having its annual charity ball and Sister Vermont can't go.'

'Why?' Rachael asked, not remotely interested in what Sister Vermont, the plastics nurse unit manager, was up to but desperate to stall this conversation.

'She's on holiday, like most of the other plastics staff. Taking the opportunity to sun themselves on the Gold Coast, no doubt, while their unit's being refurbished. She's just extended her leave, which leaves Dr Connell here short of a date.'

Rachael gave a rather wintry smile. 'I very much doubt it.'

'I am,' Hugh replied without looking up. 'It's a work function and I'd like to take one of the nursing staff to make the right noises with all the dignitaries. The type of woman I could get at this short notice probably wouldn't go down too well with the hospital board.'

'Anyway,' Rachael said irritably, 'I'd have thought the plastics unit was the last place that needed a fundraiser. From what I've seen of the patients, they're mostly loaded.'

'Ah, that's right,' Hugh said with just a trace of bitterness. 'You're the nurse who doesn't have a problem with cosmetic patients. You must remind me again, I keep forgetting.'

Rachael swallowed hard, wondering not for the first time how it had come to this. Where had all the headway they had made evaporated to, leaving them squabbling like they had on her first day?

'Besides...' Rachael busied herself with her notes. 'I'm working on Saturday night.'

'No, you're not,' Helen said with annoying cheerfulness. 'Didn't I tell you? Becky's coming from her sick leave earlier than expected. It wasn't a fracture after all just a nasty sprain. Isn't that good news?' She swivelled her eyes between the two of them, seemingly oblivious of the simmering undercurrents. 'Problem solved. You've got a date, Hugh, and Rachael gets out of night shift.' She wandered off.

Without comment Rachael carried on with her notes, determined not to be the one to break the awful silence.

'I'll send a taxi to collect you,' Hugh mumbled,

which struck Rachael as strange, not the offer to send a taxi—the sight of her in a red bikini had obviously put her humble abode way off Hugh's map—but the fact that he was mumbling. Hugh never mumbled. Hugh Connell always spoke clearly, confidently. 'I'd pick you up,' he offered by way of explanation, 'but I'm actually staying at the hotel that night, and I'll be welcoming some of the speakers long before the ball starts.'

'I'm quite capable of ringing for my own taxi. What time do you want me there?' she asked with a rather cynical laugh. 'Or, rather, what time should I be there?'

'Rachael…' He closed his eyes for a second then opened his mouth as if there was something he badly wanted to say. But nothing happened, for an age he stood there. His eyes opened finally and when they did they were troubled. She stared directly back, not giving an inch. He had hurt her, ignored her for two weeks, and now he wanted small talk. Well, he could go to hell. 'About seven,' he said finally, and, placing his pen in his top pocket, turned and left.

Picking up a file, Rachael gave a low sigh. The meticulous Hugh hadn't even bothered to finish the sentence he'd been writing, such had been his haste to get away. How were they going to survive a whole evening together?

'What did you do that for?' Rachael wasn't smiling when Helen came back with her eyes agog, a huge, expectant grin on her face.

'He needed someone to go to the ball with him,' Helen said defensively when she saw Rachael's tense face. 'I've put my foot in it, haven't I?'

'Big time,' Rachael sighed. 'Look, Helen, I know

you mean well, I know you've got it into your head that there's something there, but there just isn't. There *isn't*,' she flared when Helen gave her a doubtful look. 'You said yourself your beach charade was foolproof and look how that ended up.'

'It worked with Jack.'

'Jack loves you,' Rachael said simply. 'I'm not going to humiliate myself chasing Hugh when he blatantly doesn't want me. I was right the first time—a relationship is the last thing I need right now.'

'Probably,' Helen conceded. 'And if we were talking about any other man then I'd be the first to say it was too soon, but Hugh's a once-in-a-lifetime man, it seems a shame to let a little thing like timing get in the way.'

'I know you mean well, Helen,' Rachael said more softly, 'but it just isn't going to happen for us, and the last thing I need right now is a night on the town with the eternally unobtainable.'

Helen cringed. 'Are you still going to go?'

Rachael shrugged. 'With a bit of luck I'll come down with a healthy dose of chickenpox, but knowing my constitution I'll be pink-cheeked and disgustingly healthy. Maybe Hugh will back out,' she said hopefully. 'Maybe Sister Vermont will get sick of lording it on the Gold Coast and make an early return for the plastics ball. What do you think my chances are?'

Zero, as it turned out.

It felt strange, dressing up again after so long. An unwelcome sense of *déjà vu* assailed her as she paid the hairdresser, carefully tapping in her PIN number with her still slightly damp nails. Her hands had been shaking so much Rachael knew that any hope of a decent make-up job was useless so she had gone the whole hog and had her make-up done as well.

How many hundreds of times had she done this for Richard? How many times had she stood in front of the mirror, staring back at her sleek, sophisticated reflection and wondering if this was what it was all about. And what on earth was she getting into to-night?

Don't be silly, Rachael scolded herself, poking her tongue out between her red-painted lips. She wasn't getting into anything—it was a work do, nothing else.

Nothing else.

She still hadn't decided what to wear. Pulling open the wardrobe, rows of dresses glittered back at her. For the first time in two years she was actually spoiled for choice—there wasn't a dress she couldn't fit into, not a single zip that wouldn't pull up easily. The hell of the past year meant she finally had the figure Richard had wanted her to have. Each dress evoked a memory, a few pleasant, some agonising. Pulling out a black dress for a moment or two, Rachael closed her eyes, running her fingers along the soft velvet fabric as she remembered when she'd worn it. Remembered the soft swell of her baby beneath the fabric, the glow of knowing she was with child. It had made the endless cocktail parties, the long tedious dinners bearable.

She wanted to wear it again, wanted to feel her body as it had then, wanted her baby so badly it hurt.

Stuffing the dress back in the wardrobe with a strangled sob, she pushed her knuckles into her mouth, biting hard. She mustn't cry, mustn't go there. Tonight was about dazzling, tonight was about dancing and laughing and showing Hugh she didn't need him, didn't want him for anything more than friendship. Red-rimmed eyes and blotchy mascara weren't on the agenda. Looking in the mirror at her smeared lipstick, she let out a sigh and opened her make-up bag.

Rachael, the queen of repair jobs.

It would be written on her gravestone.

She decided on the silver. It was very sleek, very long and with dangerously thin straps. One of those dresses you bought knowing you'd never in a million years get into but daring to dream all the same.

And it looked divine.

The taxi was hooting outside, and she fought with an attack of nerves as she draped a stole over her arms, stopping for one final glimpse in the full-length mirror, torn between approval and shame as she eyed her sleek reflection. She looked every bit the trophy wife Richard had so badly wanted, every inch what she had fought so vehemently against.

The venue, set on Melbourne's south bank, was a sight in itself, dripping with luxuries as glamorous and opulent as the people swarming colourfully outside, taking advantage of the warm evening air to enjoy a casual chat or cigarette before heading inside. Rachael didn't feel out of place as she climbed the steps, her heels clicking in unison with those of the other well-dressed women, the only difference being that she didn't have a well-groomed man on her arm.

Yet.

She saw him first, standing in the massive foyer,

chatting easily with a rather ruddy-faced, elderly man, Hugh throwing his head back as he laughed at a joke. But somewhere in the middle the laughter died, the smile literally wiped off his face as his eyes met Rachael's, his hand tightening around his glass of champagne as the muscles quilted in his face.

'Rachael?' She saw his lips move, the noise in the foyer too loud to hear his voice, but the question in his eyes was obvious enough. Barely stopping to excuse himself, he crossed the foyer, beside her in an instant. 'Rachael,' he said again. This time his voice reached her ears, as delicious and familiar as a well-loved song, and she knew then there was no point denying it—the make-up, the nails, the dress, they had all been for him. His neglect and indifference might have wounded her pride but they hadn't severed her feelings. 'You look beautiful.'

She gave a nervous laugh as he kissed her on the cheek. 'I left the rubber soles at home tonight.'

He glanced down at her strappy silver sandals, taking in the cherry-red nails peeking out, the absence of a stocking seam telling Hugh that under her dress Rachael's legs were bare and undoubtedly as smooth and sheer as the enchanting silver that draped her slender body.

'Glad to hear it.' There was a slight tremor in his voice, utterly out of place with the dashing, confident man he depicted. 'You even smell wonderful.'

The same nervous laugh escaped her lips. 'I went a bit over the top with the perfume. I figured I'd be up against some pretty stiff competition.' In a totally spontaneous movement, her face neared his briefly, inhaling his overpowering yet delicious fragrance, oblivious of his clenching hands as she moved in closer. 'Seems I was right.' He didn't say anything, just stood there, swallowing hard as Rachael moved back slightly and scanned the foyer. 'What am I expected to do?' She frowned when he didn't answer. 'Hugh, what am I supposed to do tonight?'

He cleared his throat, snapping his attention to her question. 'For now just shake hands and thank people for coming. I'll make all the introductions. The small talk will come later, after the meal. With a bit of luck a few heavy envelopes might be pressed into your hand. Just pass them on to Jeffrey here.'

'Jeffrey Hillingdon, the CEO?' Rachael gave a nervous gulp.

'Our mutual boss.'

'I still don't understand,' she asked. 'What's the fundraiser for?'

He didn't answer as suddenly the floodgates of people opened. Taking her arm, he guided her to the doorway where she stood, uncomfortably aware she was in a greeting line with some of the biggest dignitaries from the hospital. 'You ready?'

She gave a nervous nod, only relaxing when one green eye shuttered in a playful wink. 'Sparkle, Rachael!' he said in a theatrical voice, reminding her so much of her old ballet teacher it made her giggle, instantly relaxing her. And just as she had realised that the make-up had all been for Hugh, the difference between him and Richard also hit her. Richard would have been nervous, falling over himself to please everyone except Rachael, barking orders to his wife from the corner of his false smile, whereas Hugh…

He just oozed charm, natural charm, his small talk witty, his jokes funny. And if they didn't go down well he shrugged and carried right on, all the while including her, every other moment checking that she was all right, ensuring that she always felt included.

There was no comparison.

And when the last guest had been greeted, when her cheeks must have been smeared like a rainbow from the lips that had briefly grazed her cheek, Rachael was smiling—a real smile, not the false one she had perfected so well. 'Time for a drink, I think,' Hugh said, taking her hand so naturally it hardly merited comment. Only as he reached the entrance to the ballroom did he seem to realise what he was doing and, shifting nervously, he removed his hand, placing it instead on the small of Rachael's back.

If the intention had been to remove any trace of intimacy, it had the opposite effect, his warm hand pressing at the base of her spine nearly propelling Rachael into orbit. Never had a glass of champagne been so gratefully received. At least it gave her something to do with her hands, with her mouth, too. Every nerve in her body seemed to be tingling; every tiny movement seemed terribly complicated all of a sudden.

'The room looks wonderful.' It was an understatement. The room was stunning, heavy white cloths draped the round tables, vast burgundy plants, all Australian natives, adorned the centre, the gleaming silver cutlery shone in the candlelight. But it all paled next to Hugh. 'Where are we sitting?' She was hoping for a dark corner, somewhere she could hide her blushes and observe the proceedings from a distance, but the heavens had obviously decided that tonight was Rachael's night. As Hugh guided her forward, with mounting horror she realised they were at the head table, the five hundred or so guests all with a view, one thousand eyes watching Rachael trying to pretend that she wasn't hopelessly in lust with her reluctant companion.

'How come we're right at the top?' she asked, hoping it was some horrible mistake.

'Because I'm the president.'

It should have been hell on earth, the most uncomfortable night of her life. But whether Hugh had decided to temporarily put their differences aside or was just having a good night, the meal turned out to be a sheer pleasure. As soon as the soup was ladled into her bowl, as soon as she spread her butter thickly on her warm roll, Rachael forgot they were the focal point of the room, forgot the five hundred pairs of eyes on them, focussing instead on the one pair that mattered. A pair of eyes that actually weren't green but more aquamarine, eyes that crinkled slightly around the edges when he smiled, which was often. For all the world it was as if they were the only couple in the room, sitting at a table for two in some secluded restaurant. And slowly as the dessert plates were cleared, as the dessert wine trickled thick and sweet down her throat, his eyes stopped smiling, the dewy sheen of lust unmistakable.

'Rachael...' His voice was hesitant. 'Thank you for coming tonight.'

She gave the tiniest of shrugs. 'It wasn't as if I had much choice.' Her eyes flicked down, suddenly aware of the intensity of his gaze. 'You didn't either.'

'But it turned out all right?'

Rachael nodded, taking a grateful sip of her wine. 'It's been great.'

'After…' Hugh coughed slightly, covering his mouth with hand. 'I mean, when I've done my duty, so to speak, will you stay?'

She looked up, suddenly confused. 'Stay?'

He smiled, realising what he had said. 'I meant for coffee, brandy, whatever. Maybe a walk along the river. I'm going to be pretty tied up for a while and I don't want you disappearing on me.' The smile faded, his voice suddenly serious. 'I think we both need to talk.'

'We are talking,' Rachael pointed out, stalling, knowing where this was leading, thrilled and terrified at the same time.

'You know what I mean.'

She nodded, a bubble of excitement welling in her stomach, and as the lights dimmed, as the attention of the room focussed on the top table, her excitement turned to pride as Hugh stood up, his deep, silken voice caressing the room, holding the audience captive, as he told them the details of his work, giving them and, more pointedly, Rachael a glimpse of the compassionate man behind that smooth smile. And when a brief presentation started, Rachael gasped along with the guests as she saw the dark little faces that filled the screen, horribly scarred and deformed, the soft music in the background enhancing the tragedy that marred these children's lives.

The horror of burns untreated.

'At this point I want to thank you all. Thank you for parting with your money, for donating your time by being here tonight. Thank the hospitals that provide scarce bed space for these overseas children, the accountants who factor it into their budgets, the nurses who care for them, the surgeons whose skills transform these children and the airlines that fly them here. But as we sit here feeling pretty pleased with ourselves I ask that we don't get too comfortable. That we remember this is just the tip of the iceberg.'

He flicked a button in his hand and a brown-eyed girl stared back, smiling shyly at the camera. 'Those of you who attended last year will remember me talking about Kimbi, the little girl who fell into a fire and whose lips and eyes were fused closed.' A far less appealing picture replaced the picture and Rachael felt the colour drain from her face. The features were almost unrecognisable from the girl before. 'Today, thanks to the generosity of people like yourselves, those eyes are open. Those lips, which could only manage the tiniest sips of rice water, now talk and laugh and share in happy meals with her family. Of course she has scars—this little girl has undergone twelve operations after all—but I think it's fair to say that she's pretty much unrecognisable from the little girl we spoke about last year. If you notice my voice soften when I talk about Kimbi, I make no apology—she has a special place in everyone's heart.'

His green eyes worked the room and there was a tiny pause as he took a sip of water.

'Kimbi is coming back on Monday for what I hope will be her final operation. The last time I spoke to her, with the help of her translator, Kimbi told me that she wanted to be a doctor.' Hugh shuffled his notes and looked up again. 'I don't have any children, and my speciality certainly isn't child psychology, but I'm pretty sure that when most ten-year-olds say they want to be doctor, it's a rather empty statement. But not Kimbi. If any little girl is going to make something of her life, I'm sure it will be her, and who knows what she might go on to achieve? How the seed we've sown by giving her this chance might somehow reap rewards far greater than we first dared to dream.'

His voice was louder suddenly, forcing those that were reaching for a drink, starting to murmur amongst themselves, to turn their attention back to the speaker.

'It would be so easy to leave it there, to pat ourselves on the back and order another bottle of red, but it doesn't just end there. There are no fire-guards in the remote villages of Papua New Guinea, no central heating or microwave ovens. These horrific injuries are commonplace. Children are children, they play near the fires, they fall and then they burn.' His expressive eyes worked the room. 'They burn,' he said again more quietly. 'And it's up to us to take it from there.'

The applause was deafening, and as Hugh sat down modestly it was Rachael who clapped the loudest, her palms red by the time Hugh put a hand on her arm to stop her.

'You were wonderful.' Her eyes were shining with admiration. 'Hugh, I just never realised…'

'It's no big deal.' He shrugged, a tiny blush spreading over his face as Rachael begged to differ.

'It's a huge deal! I feel awful.' She gave him a playful thump. 'Why didn't you tell me? Why did you let me bang on about narcissistic tendencies when all time you were doing this type of work?'

'I was waiting for the right moment.' He smiled, a devilish smile that made her insides melt. The hot breath of his whisper tickled her ears, sending a million tiny volts through her system. 'Aiming for maximum impact! Anyway, I love a woman on a guilt trip.'

Rachael sat through the rest of the speeches, achingly aware of Hugh next to her, hugging the knowledge of their talk yet to come like a secret treasure to be opened later. Tonight she had learned so much about him. That he was good-looking and talented were common knowledge, but the depth of his compassion, the way those skills were utilised—for Rachael it was nothing short of a revelation.

'Dance?'

She could have blamed it on the champagne, blamed it on her impossibly high heels—the fact her knees seemed so impossibly weak and her legs so horrendously unsteady as she crossed the room—but it left Rachael with no choice but to melt into his body, to let him guide her to the music. To feel him strong and lean beneath her trembling fingers as he held her close.

'Your speech was marvellous,' she said approvingly.

'They all went well.'

'Yours was definitely the best,' she said proudly. 'I think you were easily the most persuasive.'

'And I think you've had too much champagne.'

'Am I embarrassing you?' she asked, quickly pulling away, but he just laughed and pulled her closer.

'You *never* embarrass me. But your bias and sud-

den admiration has to be put down to something.
I'm guessing it's the champagne.'

'Maybe a bit,' she agreed. 'And if I am a bit tipsy
then I'm allowed to ask silly questions.'

'Ask away.'

'Why don't you fancy me?' She felt him stiffen.
Suddenly they weren't moving any more, just standing in the middle of the dance floor.

'Rachael.' That authoritative note was back, that
warning tone that said not to push things, but
Rachael was past caring, past heeding the warning
bells. She adored him, wanted him, needed him and,
right here, right now, Rachael wanted to know
where she had gone so wrong.

'Why do you want to just be friends?' The longest
silence followed, apart from the band, of course,
apart from five hundred people milling about in a
ballroom, but as she held her breath, awaiting his
answer, the night was just about the two of them.

'I don't.'

She heard the slight waver in his voice as he imparted those delicious words and it was all the en-
couragement she needed, gave her enough ammu-
nition to fire for the skies.

'So why haven't you ever kissed me?'

'I thought I was doing the right thing…'

'By not kissing me?' Her eyes dragged up to his,
holding his gaze, utterly refusing to let it be. 'Didn't
you want to?'

'Rachael,' he said again, a note of exasperation
in his voice. 'You know I wanted to.'

She shook her head and only her eyes stayed still,
one lock of hair escaping the carefully slicked

chignon. His hand reached up, smoothing the tendril behind her ear, tracing the elegant line of her neck.

'Then why didn't you?

'Why—?' She never got to finish.

His mouth was on hers then, she felt the slight roughness of his chin. An eleven p.m. shadow, Rachael thought as she felt his heavy mouth, his cool tongue that tasted of champagne moving slowly, languorously. His kiss, his touch was everything she had dreamt of, everything she had desired, and there wasn't even a notion of hesitancy, even a glimmer of doubt as she kissed him back. And when he'd finished kissing her, when any longer with their lips entwined would have bordering on indecency, he pulled reluctantly away, staring down at her flushed, radiant face, a slow smile on his newly kissed lips.

'Better now?'

She nodded, his kiss her answer.

'It's heavenly here.' With a sigh she leant against him. She loved the smell of him, loved the fact he used too much aftershave. Hugh Connell was too much, much too much to be close to and not be moved. He was excessive, dangerous and tonight…

He was hers.

'You should see the rooms.' His arms were wrapped around her and her body reacted to his touch. Her nipples, jutting through the silk fabric of her dress, were almost painful. But it hadn't been an invitation and Rachael had to bite on her lip to stop a provocative reply as he carried on talking. 'I went to have a shower, nothing dangerous in that, or so I thought. I nearly took my eye out.' She gave a gurgle of laughter as he continued, 'The jets come from all sides.'

'I'd love to see them.'

It was Hugh that pulled back then, his eyes burning into hers, the tiniest hint of a teasing question in them.

She felt brave, *he* made her feel brave. Taking a deep breath, her eyes didn't flicker away, just held him right there. 'I think we could both use a cool shower.' She swallowed. Her blush had nothing to do with embarrassment, just the rosy glow of arousal. 'Don't you?'

'Hell, Rachael,' he croaked, half laughing, half cursing. 'How am I supposed to make it back to the table now?'

She nestled against him, laughing at his embarrassment. 'Looks like we're going to have to just keep right on dancing.'

There was something incredibly sexy about a deserted ballroom. The lipstick on the glasses, the tired staff listlessly cleaning up, the popped balloons and slowly wilting flowers. Or maybe it had something to do with the two of them sitting at the table, oblivious of the pointed stares from the waiters as they laughed at each other's jokes, spread cheese on crackers and fed each other like lovers.

'Let's walk,' Hugh suggested.

'Let's not,' Rachael grumbled. All she wanted was for him to take her across the magnificent foyer up to his splendid room, lay her on the bed and make love to her.

'We need to talk.'

CHAPTER NINE

ONLY in Melbourne.

Maybe in a hundred other cities in the world you could walk along the river barefoot in a ballgown, holding hands, on the threshold of the love affair of a lifetime, but Melbourne was one of the few places in the world you could do it in utter safety, barely meriting a glance. Jeans or jewels were treated with the same friendly politeness. They shared a smile as they sat at an outdoor café, accepting the coffee the waitress placed in front of them.

'I hope that's the groom.' Rachael followed Hugh's gaze and grinned as she watched a bride in full regalia pull off her shoes then jump onto her husband's lap.

'You asked why I didn't kiss you.'

Suddenly she felt incredibly shy. Maybe she had instigated all this, but that had been when in a ballroom full of people, the best part of a bottle of champagne doing unmentionable things to her usually shredded confidence. Two coffees later and suddenly Rachael didn't feel so brave any more.

'Do you remember your first day back?'

'Of course I do.'

'Do you remember what earrings you were wearing, what colour hair tie you had on? How many pens you had in your pocket?'

She stared at him, dumbfounded, no idea where he was heading.

'I do,' he said simply. 'I remember every tiny
detail. The second I stood up and turned around and
saw you, something happened, Rachael. I don't
know if it was love at first sight, but if it wasn't it
was a damned good imitation.' He stirred his coffee
as she sat there, trembling. 'I've never reacted so
violently to anyone. Hell, Rachael, I get on with
everyone, and there I was, ten minutes after meeting
you, on the verge of losing my temper.

'Then you told me about Amy.'

She watched the froth in her café latte disperse,
fiddled with her teaspoon and tore at yet another
packet of sugar, which she slowly drizzled over her
drink.

'I knew then that I had to take things gently. Yes,
I was attracted to you, yes, I wanted to get to know
you, but you'd been through so much already, I just
thought a relationship probably wasn't on your
agenda.'

'It wasn't,' Rachael admitted half to herself, then
added more forcibly, 'In fact, it was the furthest
thing from my mind.' The softest sound escaped her
lips, a gentle, thoughtful sigh. 'Then you came
along.'

'Sitting in that restaurant…' he gestured along the
river, pointing her thoughts to where it had all be-
gun, not so long ago yet a lifetime away '…I
thought I could do it, thought I could be there for
you, and, I'm sorry if this sounds presumptuous, I
wanted to be the one to be there for you. Wanted to
make things better.'

'To be the good guy?' She shook her head when
he didn't answer. 'No one can make it better, Hugh,'
she said without a trace of self-pity. 'Not even you.'

'I don't believe that. I know life can never be perfect for you, I know there will always be a part of you that's grieving, desolate, but I truly believe it can still be better.'

He sounded so sure, so confident she almost believed him.

'I thought you needed a friend.' Hugh's hand was edging over the table. With a flash of impatience he jerked the teaspoon away and grabbed at her hand, commanding her to concentrate. 'And, fool that I am, I thought I could be that friend, put the attraction I undoubtedly felt on the back burner and be there for you. And if in time something grew, then all the better.' He closed his eyes and Rachael waited in silence for him to continue. 'You come with a lot of baggage, Rachael.'

Pulling her hand away, she reached again for the spoon. 'Sorry about that,' she said sarcastically, but his hand reached across for her chin this time, forcing her eyes up to his.

'You've nothing to apologise for, and I don't care a damn about your past, not in that sense anyway. What I care about is you. I can't be a friend to you, Rachael. When you were hissing and spitting, I could just about manage it, but when you relaxed, when you started to unwind...' He let out a long sigh. 'Driving you home that night, I knew for a fact I couldn't be what you needed.'

'So I wasn't imagining things?' She gave a low laugh. 'How do you know what I need? How can you know when you haven't even asked?'

'The way I feel about you, Rachael, it isn't going to be a casual fling. I'm crazy about you, you're all I think about.'

'Honestly?' She blinked a couple of times. 'But you seemed so...so detached. All that talk about being friends...'

'Rachael, I've been going crazy trying to be nice, trying to keep my feelings hidden. Sitting with you in the movies, sharing a bottle of wine, you've no idea how hard it's been to pretend I don't want you.' Hugh gave her a smile. 'Guess what? I hate cricket, can't stand the wretched game, but, watching you rub in that oil, it was either fall in love with the game—and quickly—or risk taking you to bed then and there.'

'Honestly?'

'Honestly.' His voice was suddenly serious. 'I don't want you to regret anything. I don't want you to regret tonight, for it to be an impulse thing because we're both looking good and have had a bit too much to drink.'

'There's nothing impulsive about my feelings, Hugh.' It was Rachael who now took his hand. 'You know that picnic basket? Do you remember how I nearly jumped out of my skin when you offered to take it out to the car for me?' She watched him frown as he recalled the incident. 'Well, guess what was in it?'

'Chicken.' He shrugged. 'Chicken and wine.'

'Uh-uh,' Rachael shook her head. 'Two condoms.'

'Condoms?' The bride and groom sitting nearby stopped kissing and looked over, along with the rest of the café. Hugh recovered quickly and gave her a deep, intimate smile, the sort of smile that had her stomach turning somersaults. 'Two wouldn't have been enough, you know.'

'I would hope not.' Rachael felt like picking up the table, picking it up and hurling it into the river such was her need to be beside him. But Hugh was right. They needed to talk, needed to get things out in the open, and it wasn't quite finished yet. 'They're not mutually exclusive.'

His forehead creased as she tentatively continued, 'Friends can be lovers, too.'

But he shook his head. 'You know what I mean. I want you, Rachael.' His words caused a warm glow to spread through her, shielding her from the inevitable 'but' that was about to come. 'What if Richard comes back?'

'He's not going to.'

'You were together eight years, Rachael, that has to count for something. You've just lost a baby… Surely that's enough to test even the strongest marriage.'

'It wasn't a strong marriage,' she reasoned. 'Amy's death just brought it to a head. In some ways it destroyed me, while in others it strengthened me.'

'That evening, when I came round after Sheila died, you were wearing his shirt.'

'So?'

He gave her a long look. 'It just seemed…I don't know, intimate, I guess.'

'You think that means I still want him?'

'I don't know,' he answered honestly. 'I just don't know what to think where you're concerned, Rachael. You don't exactly come with a user manual.'

'It was an old shirt,' Rachael said, a smile spreading on her face as she watched Hugh's reaction, understanding how such a seemingly insignificant detail would be enough to compound his doubts at such a vulnerable time. 'I don't even think he ever wore it—it probably wasn't expensive enough for him. I think I've even done the gardening in it. Honestly, Hugh, I wasn't having a melancholy night in, dreaming about Richard. It was you I was thinking about.

'You,' she said again softly. 'And, if you must know, you're *all* that I seem to have been thinking about recently.'

'Rachael.' Richard's voice, incredulous, tentative, was like an unwelcome ghost, and she literally froze as Hugh looked up in stunned disbelief.

Only in Melbourne.

Only here would your ex-husband be strolling hand in hand along the river with his date. A city it might be, but it wasn't quite big enough to get lost in.

'Richard.' In a flurry of nervousness she jumped up. 'Hugh, this is Richard, my—'

Hugh didn't even bother to be polite. 'I think I get the picture.'

'You're looking marvellous,' Richard enthused. 'Marvellous.' He eyed her up and down with undisguised admiration. 'You've lost so much weight.'

Those five little words were enough to snap Rachael back to attention and she sat back down, trying to catch Hugh's eye to give him an apologetic smile. But he was staring fixedly ahead, not even bothering to attempt small talk.

The desperate socialite, Richard attempted to flog a dead horse. 'Beautiful night. We've just been to Grant Hisslop's engagement—you remember Grant?' He seemed to remember then that he had company. 'This is Susie.' His partner flashed a toothy white smile, her face bored and impassive. 'So, where have you two been?' Richard asked in a friendly voice that was so false it set the hairs on Rachael's neck on end.

'At a fundraising ball,' she mumbled. When the silence dragged on painfully she desperately tried to fill it. 'Hugh's a plastic surgeon—they're raising money for overseas children.'

'Splendid.' Richard smiled. 'So it's a work thing, then?' There was no mistaking the edge to his voice, and the silence she had tried to fill before widened to an abyss as she realised the implication to his question.

'No,' she said slowly, her eyes darting to Hugh who sat with a slightly questioning look on his face as he awaited her response. 'I was there *with* Hugh.'

'Come on, Wichard,' Susie simpered in a baby voice, tugging at his sleeve as she made to go. 'My feet are positively killing me.'

'Yes, quite.' He gave a shrug. 'Better be getting back. The other partners will be wondering where I got to. Lovely to see you again, Rachael.'

Only when he was gone, when even if he turned around he wouldn't be able to see her, did Rachael bury her burning face in her hands and moan. 'Oh, God, I am so, so sorry,' she groaned. Parting her fingers a fraction she was stunned, utterly floored to see Hugh nearly falling off his chair, laughing.

'Don't,' she squealed. 'I'm so embarrassed.'

'Why?' he roared, wiping a tear from his face with the back of his hand. 'What better time to meet your ex-husband than when you're sitting with a

gorgeous blond toy boy, looking fabulous? If anyone was embarrassed, it was him.'

'Do you think?' Rachael asked, only then daring
to peel her hands away from her face. 'That Susie
didn't look too fazed.'

'She was spitting chips,' Hugh said assuredly.

'Well, she didn't look it.'

'Susie couldn't look anything other than impassive with a face full of Botox. I can assure you,
darling, she wasn't happy.'

Darling. That small endearment brought the
whole world into perspective. She was sitting, on a
balmy summer night, with the most wonderful, gorgeous man who could make even the most awkward
difficult situation funny all of a sudden. Ten
Richards could have appear right now and she
couldn't have cared less.

'Women like that are ten a penny, Rachael. If
that's what you want to look like, book in for an
appointment.' His hand was back now, holding hers
tenderly. 'It's you I want, exactly as you are.'

'Honestly?'

He nodded, slowly, definitely. 'Yep.'

'And what's this about a toy boy? Just how old
are you exactly?'

'Thirty-five.'

'Hardly a toy boy,' Rachael said with a grin.

'Don't ruin the picture,' he whispered. 'When you
tell the story later, it has to be perfect.'

Rachael swallowed, 'It already is.'

Pulling out a note, Hugh slapped it on to the table
and stood up, holding his hand out for her to join
him. 'Come on, *Wachael*, there's a certain part of
my anatomy that's positively killing me.'

*   *   *

The water did jet from all angles, hot, sharp jets hitting their tightly coiled bodies, knocking the breath out of them as their lips met, sated with desire. One by one Hugh pulled the pins out of Rachael's long chocolate locks, massaging shampoo as the goo and the mousse slipped down her shoulders. He gently rubbed every last trace of make-up off her flushed face as he kissed each slender shoulder, every last hidden crevice.

And Rachael... The soap slipped through her fingers, bouncing onto the floor unnoticed as she worked the rich lather through the blond mat of his chest, working the suds downward till she held him slippery and warm and splendid in her trembling hands. Massaging more gently now but with a deeper urgency, she felt his hands on her shoulders gently but firmly pushing her down and she knelt on the floor, running her tongue along the inside of his muscular thigh working her mouth upwards as she felt his muscles tense, the water cascading around her as she took him into the soft warmth of her mouth. His fingers tightened in her hair and she felt him shudder, his broad back resting against the cool tiles, his thighs rhythmically rubbing against her swollen breasts as she took him ever deeper. Never had she thought she could get so much pleasure from giving. Her own body was trembling with desire, the blood rushing to her groin like mercury, her temples pounding as they both hovered on the brink of oblivion.

'Rachael,' he gasped, his voice almost drowned by the gushing water. Pulling her reluctantly up, he held her against him. 'Not yet.' His voice was a hoarse, reluctant whisper. In one lithe motion he hoisted her up, kicking the glass door of the shower open. Not bothering to turn off the taps, he carried her through to the bedroom then, sitting her on the bed, he wrapped her in a towel, drying her gently.

Without the make-up, without the skilfully blow-dried hair, she looked almost childlike. Like a child pulled from a storm. He dried her, his hands working every inch of her, behind her ears, between her toes, massaging her scalp with the thick white towel in the most sensual of massages, working the towel in small circular motions up her leg behind her knee till she lay back on the bed gasping in anticipation, till every inch of her was dry.

Everywhere except the dark warm sweet place that was as moist and welcoming as he knew it would be. The towel forgotten, he explored her with infinite finesse, tender skill, his tongue flicking till she moaned with frenzied desire, unable to hold on a second longer. He sensed from her urgency that now was not the time to be holding back, and neither could he.

With one powerful thrust he slipped inside her, groaning with ecstasy as she gripped him tighter, moving with her, for her, pushing her further and longer than she'd ever thought possible, until all that mattered was this moment pushing away the dark clouds the silver lining of oblivion, their primitive needs fulfilled.

The joining of man and woman.

'Don't go.' Rachael pulled him back but he kissed the tip of her nose and slipped out of the bed.

'I'm only turning off the taps.'

The short time it took saw her climb into the bed,

a smile shining on her face as she surveyed the chaos they had created in the room. And then Hugh was walking towards her and her heart melted all over again. Mentally pinching herself that this man adored her, had made love to her, and from the glorious length of his manhood wanted her over again.

'I thought union rules stated a ten-minute break between shifts,' she said with a breathless laugh as he climbed into bed beside her, nuzzling her neck, his body stretching beside her, primed and deliciously ready.

'Maybe in the public sector,' he drawled in that effortless superior voice that made her insides turn to liquid. 'But you're on my team now and, I warn you, I make a merciless, demanding boss.'

'Sounds wonderful,' she murmured as she slipped into his arms, submitting again to the mastery of his touch. 'In fact, it sounds just about perfect.'

CHAPTER TEN

'COME down to breakfast.' Hugh was standing knotting his tie, just as Rachael had imagined that day in the treatment room, and the vision was just as perfect as her imagination had been.

Better even.

'They won't bite.'

'Maybe not,' Rachael conceded. 'But I hardly think a crumpled silver ballgown and fluffy hair are really on.'

'We're at south bank. There are shops everywhere, it will be no problem to nip out and get you something.'

Rachael laughed. 'On a Sunday morning? Come on, Hugh, only the tourist shops will be open now and I hardly think a T-shirt with a koala bear on it and a pair of I-love-Australia boxers will exactly endear them to me.'

'I just don't want you to think I'm abandoning you. I can give it a miss, the world won't stop if I skip breakfast.' Which was so like him, Rachael realised so straightforward, no guarded reasons, no second-guessing his motives, a world away from Richard and his corporate games.

'What, and miss the pats on the back for last night's speech? You go, Hugh. Take as long as you have to, I'll be fine.' Picking up the folder by the bedside, she cast a ravenous eye over the menu. 'More than fine actually. I love eggs Benedict.'

'I'd rather be here with you.' His words were soft, but there was something in the seductive drawl in which they were delivered that made her eyes flick up.

'I'll still be here when you're finished.' The reference was to breakfast but as they held each other's eyes she knew the meaning was deeper. Last night had been so much more than a fling, a release of sexual tension. It had been a coming together, a brief but heady interlude on a much longer journey. 'Your work is important, Hugh.'

His lips tugged at the edges, teasing her with a smile as his eyes raked over her body, barely covered by the rumpled sheet. 'So I've finally managed to impress you, huh? You finally realise that I'm not just about breast enlargements and Botox.'

'Yes,' she admitted. 'I'm suitably impressed.' Her light-hearted response grew more serious. 'I really am,' Rachael admitted. 'And it's important that you go to the breakfast. Carry on the work, Hugh, those children need all the help they can get. Your speech really made people sit up and take notice, there was hardly a dry eye in the house.'

'Except yours.'

His two words stilled her. The teasing game had ended and they were on the verge of something deeper, somewhere dangerous, somewhere Rachael wouldn't, couldn't go. She felt the mattress indent as he lowered himself beside her, pulling her hand to his. She felt like Hugh was a hospital visitor sitting there fully dressed as she lay there vulnerable, exposed. A visitor who felt they had to ask all the right questions, only there wasn't the saving grace here of the bell, no ward sister to shoo him away when the questions got too much.

'I've never seen you cry, Rachael.'

She must have read the breakfast menu ten times now but still she worked her way through it again. 'The pink grapefruit juice sounds nice.'

'Rachael, put the menu down.'

She tried to joke her way out of it, wrapping her hands around her mouth in a poor imitation of a megaphone. 'Put down the menu and come out with your emotions in the air.'

'I'm not joking, Rachael. Put down the menu.'

'Why?' she answered smartly, her voice firm and steady.

'So that you can stop avoiding me. I've never seen you cry,' he said again.

'So from that you conclude that you don't know me?' She gave a rather shrill laugh. 'What? Do men need to see a woman broken, at her absolute worst, to make them feel better?' she asked angrily as he sat there silently. 'We've only know each other a few weeks, and might I point out I haven't seen you sobbing into a handkerchief too many times?'

'I haven't lost a baby.' The words hung in the air, the horrible truth summing up so very neatly the sheer hell she'd been through. 'I haven't just come back from maternity leave and had to face the world. And, yes, we might have only met relatively recently, but we've been through quite a bit,' he said gently. 'You told me about Amy, your divorce, Sheila's death, a couple of movies that just about set me off, even meeting up with your ex-husband, and I've never seen even a hint of a tear.' His eyes were burning into her and she couldn't bear it, couldn't bear that he might see her so exposed and see the murky depths of her despair. 'Hell, Rachael, when I hear what you've been through, *I* feel like crying.'

'Maybe I'm not the emotional kind,' she responded flippantly, picking up the menu again, but Hugh grabbed it from her, tossing it across the bed.

'Rubbish.' His hand gripped her wrist. 'You're the most emotional woman I've ever met, and if I needed any proof, last night proved it beyond a shadow of doubt.' He ran his free hand through his hair and let out a ravaged sigh. 'I want you to know that I understand.' The dubious look that darted across her taut face didn't go unnoticed. 'Or as much as I can,' he corrected. 'I know you come with a lot of pain, Rachael. I want you to know that I understand that it can't all be fun and romance and making love, that there will be dark times.' He hesitated for a second. 'It will be her birthday soon, won't it?'

A tiny forward movement of her head was all the answer he was going to get. 'I know that if we're going to make this work, and I want this to work more than you know, Rachael, then we have to trust each other, maybe open up a bit earlier and sooner than other couples. I want to be there for you in the bad times, too. I can't bear to think of you crying alone.'

'I don't cry alone,' Rachael said quickly, ignoring his puzzled expression as she continued. 'I don't cry at all, in fact, so you don't have to worry about me.'

'But you must, after all you've been through…'

'Where would it get me?'

'So you've never cried about Amy?' His voice was filled with sheer bewilderment.

'I cried the day she was born,' Rachael admitted. 'The same day that she died. And I haven't shed a tear since.'

'What about the funeral?'

Rachael closed her eyes, battling with the painful memories of that bleak, dark day. 'No,' she admitted.

'When you left Richard?'

A second's silence and she briefly shook her head.

'Do you know why I don't cry?' Her voice was rising, her eyes flashing angrily at him for daring to unearth her reluctant secret. 'Do you really want to know why?' He nodded calmly, ignoring the anger in her voice, sitting patiently as she struggled to continue. 'Because I'm scared.'

'Of what?'

She swallowed and took a deep breath, her eyes darting around the room, looking anywhere but at Hugh. 'Because I honestly believe that if I give in, if I start crying, I won't be able to stop.' Her eyes found his. 'It's as simple as that.' She took a deep, cleansing breath and forced a rather watery smile. 'You'd better go. The guests will be waiting.'

'Let them wait.' He pulled her towards him, held her stiff and unyielding in her arms as she tried to wriggle away.

'Don't, Hugh,' she pleaded. His touch, his tenderness was the last thing she needed now if she were to stay in control.

'Rachael, I'm here,' he said, his voice thick with emotion. 'I'm here for you, and one day, maybe soon, maybe ages away but someday, when you're ready to let it out, I'll still be here.' He stroked her hair, softly, tenderly, and he held her as any man would have held the woman he loved, but for the first time his touch wasn't sexual, just loving, comforting and infinitely safe. 'And when you stop crying…' He felt her stiffen but carried on talking gently. 'Which I promise that you will, I'll still be here, and we'll move on together.'

She let him hold her then, relaxed her body against his, revelling in the warmth of the quiet strength in his body, allowing herself to be comforted. 'Please,' she said finally when she could hold out no more, when the tears were only a breath away. 'Please, Hugh, just go.'

Hugh let her go, reluctantly but without argument.

The offer was on the table—it wasn't for him to dictate the terms.

Thank heavens for late checkout. For those delicious extra four hours between ten and two when the bed remained unmade where the newspapers Rachael had been languorously reading on Hugh's return were tossed to the floor as he arrived back from his breakfast meeting, impatient and aroused, his casual attire discarded more easily than the formal wear the previous night. Their love-making was more leisurely this time, deliciously new still but with a heady touch of familiarity as they retraced each other's erogenous zones.

'We're going to be the talk of the street.' Rachael laughed as they neared her house. Every husband in suburbia seemed to have chosen today to mow his lawn, and a speedy dash up the garden path in her silver frock was going to raise more than a few eyebrows.

'I've got a blanket in the boot,' Hugh said. 'I could always put on my white coat and carry you in. They'll think you had a fall last night or something.'

'Since when did the health service offer door-to-door service?'

The motor idled as he turned to her. 'OK, forget the blanket. They'll think I'm carrying you over the threshold.'

'How about I hold my head high and just plain walk? I don't have to explain myself to my neighbours.' She watched the colour literally drain out of his face, the laughter die on his lips as his knuckles clutched the steering-wheel. With a surge of nervous energy she turned her head to where he was staring.

'What about Richard?' His words were like pistol shots. 'Do you have to explain yourself to him?'

She couldn't believe what she was seeing. She didn't even think Richard knew where she lived, yet there he was, pacing around on the garden path, *her* garden path. 'I definitely don't have to explain myself to him,' Rachael answered with a steely determination that belied the dive her stomach had taken. Today had been so perfect, too perfect, and now it was payback time. 'Hugh, I've no idea what he's doing here.'

'I have.' His jaw was clenched so tight his mouth barely moved as he spoke. 'He wants you, Rachael.'

'He doesn't.' She gave a nervous laugh. 'It's over.'

'Is it?' The pistol shots were fired again. 'For a marriage that's over, he seems to be around one helluva lot.'

'I haven't seen him in months,' she pleaded. 'Hugh, you have to believe me.'

'Believe this.' His voice was ominous and there was no mistaking his jealousy. 'Get rid of him, Rachael. I can't do this.'

'Do what?'

'This…' He gestured wildly in the air. 'I won't be a fling on the rebound.'

'But you're not,' she replied. 'You're overreacting.'

'The ink on your divorce papers is barely dry, it's near the anniversary of your daughter's death and Richard is on your doorstep. I saw the way he looked at you last night, and he wants you.'

'But I don't want him.'

Her words seemed to reach him and Hugh let out a long ragged sigh. Rachael blinked a couple of times, scarcely able to believe the change in him, the proprietorial way he was behaving, and yet she understood it.

'Then get rid of him.' He watched as she opened the car door. 'I'll wait here.'

There wasn't much mowing going on in suburbia now. Every lawnmower in earshot must have been turned off as she stepped out of the car. But, then, who could blame them? Hugh's black sports car was pretty eye-catching and a woman in a silver ball-gown at three p.m. was quite a sight. Toss in an ex-husband waiting on the doorstep and, hell, why not call the wife and kids out to have a look?

'Richard,' she started angrily, striding toward him, but he beat her to it.

'I'm sorry.' He motioned to the car. 'I didn't

mean to turn up while he was here. I don't want to cause you any problems.'

'Well, you are,' she said pointedly. 'Just what do you want? What on earth made you come here?' Her voice was rising now and Richard put his finger up to his lips.

'Please, Rachael, everyone's looking…'

'Let them look,' she snarled. 'I'm not your wife any more, Richard, you can't tell me to be quiet and blend in any more. If I want to make a scene then I damn well will.'

'I need to talk.'

'I don't want to hear it.'

'Please,' he begged. 'I'm not coping.'

His words stunned her, literally stunned her into silence, the smart, fiery response dying on her lips as she looked at him, really looked. And he looked terrible. His face was an unhealthy grey, there were dark rings under his eyes and for someone as proud and correct as Richard the admission that life wasn't perfect was a shock in itself.

'Can we go inside?'

Dumbly she nodded, her dark locks falling forward as she scrabbled in her bag for her keys.

Amy.

It was the only thing on her mind. How many nights had she sat with her memory box on her lap, staring at the photos, running the ribboned lock of her daughter's hair through her fingers? Only yesterday, hadn't she held the velvet of her maternity dress in her hand and held onto a memory? She didn't have much but she did have proof. Tangible proof that Amy had existed.

And what did Richard have? Nothing.

And if, after all this time, he wanted to talk, to share in the painfully few memories then who was she to deny him? Amy had a mother and father, she deserved one dignified afternoon in her memory.

Hugh would have to understand.

Hugh!

'Wait inside.' She literally flew down the path to the car, but as she did so she heard the engine start up. Breathless, she careered to a halt by the driver's window, and by the look on Hugh's face she half expected him to drive off. But he seemed to relent and the glass slid down, Rachael's face anxious as she peered inside.

'Hugh, please, don't go like this.'

'Like what, Rachael?' He was staring fixedly ahead.

'Angry.' She gestured in the air. 'Upset.'

'What do you want, a cheerful wave and a kiss for luck, or perhaps you want me to wait outside, sit here until you've finished your little tête-à-tête?'

'No.' Nervously she chewed her bottom lip, unsure what to say. The truth was she didn't really know what she wanted Hugh to do. 'I'm just asking you not to drive off angry, to try to understand that I need to talk to him. I mean, Richard needs to talk. He's not coping. It's just for today, Hugh, it really is a one-off.'

'Please,' he scoffed, his fingers drumming on the wheel. 'I mean it, Rachael, I'm not sharing you. It's him or me. He's in or out your life as far I'm concerned, not somewhere in the middle, and if that makes me arrogant or jealous then I'll put my hand up and take the blame. He hurt you,' he rasped. 'He

nearly destroyed you, yet with one crook of his finger you open the door to him.'

'We were together for eight years,' she pleaded,
but her attempt at placating Hugh only seemed to
incense him further.

'And we've been together one night.' He gave a
low, bitter laugh. 'I get the picture.'

'It's not that.'

'Then what? What is he doing in your house
while I'm sitting in the car?'

She opened her mouth, then snapped it closed
again. How could she expect him to understand?
How could anyone understand? Hugh had offered
her a sympathetic ear, a free rein to talk about her
beloved daughter, but...Richard was, always would
be Amy's father. All she wanted was one poignant
afternoon, the chance to talk about her labour and
pregnancy with someone who had been there, to talk
to someone who had held Amy, knew what she had
been, what she could have been. In time she would
explain to Hugh, but not now, not with the engine
running and a street full of neighbours. For now he'd
just have to do with the condensed version.

'He wants to talk about Amy.' She watched for
Hugh's reaction but his features were unreadable.

'Are you sure about that?' There was a sneer in
Hugh's voice that just didn't belong. 'Are you sure
he doesn't just know what buttons to push?'

'That's a terrible thing to say.' Incensed, she
stepped back then thought better and angrily swung
her face to confront him head on. 'We had a child
together.'

'Did he hold you then, Rachael? Did he comfort
you, try to understand? No, he signed you up for

the bloody gym and told you to pull yourself together. He wants you back, Rachael. I'm a man and
I know what he's thinking. He's seen you with me
and he doesn't like it.'

'I'm going inside,' she said firmly, but her resolve
wavered at the final hurdle. 'Is that it, then, is that
us finished?'

If her eyes hadn't been screwed tightly shut she'd
have seen his face soften slightly.

'No,' he said after an age, his voice tired, almost
weary. 'I'll come over tonight but, heaven help me,
Rachael, if he's still there you can forget it.'

The engine roared into life and he sped off so
quickly she was left literally standing in a puff of
smoke. With a proud toss of her head she walked
along the street and up her path, listening as the
mowers purred back into life, resisting the urge to
shout that the show was over as she marched into
the house.

Annoyingly, Richard was making coffee.

Extremely annoyingly, in fact. There he was in
her kitchen, filling up *her* mugs from *her* kettle as
if it was the most natural thing in the world.

'I can't find the sweeteners,' he said by way of
greeting.

'I don't have any,' Rachael said with a distinct
edge to her voice. 'It's the real thing here, Richard.
I take two sugars now, two large sugars.' He
spooned them in without comment, which must have
hurt, Rachael thought with a wry smile, and as he
pulled open the fridge she leant back against the
kitchen wall. 'If you're looking for the low-fat milk,
there isn't any.'

'Rachael, please, I didn't come here for this.'

Suddenly she felt stupid, stupid and petty. In the months they had been apart she had somehow distorted him into some sort of calorie-counting monster, an ogre, but now here he was, and all he looked like was Richard, a little bit more jaded, a bit shabbier, definitely more tired, but the monster she had envisaged just didn't exist.

'He seemed pretty put out,' Richard said, handing her the mug, which she took without thanks.

'Do you blame him? Ex-husbands don't make the most welcome guest on a Sunday afternoon.'

'So it's serious, then?'

It would have been so much easier to have said no. To tell Richard that it was early days yet, far too soon to be talking things up, but it would have been a lie. She and Hugh had shared so much in so little time. She had slept with him, the only man whose bed she had shared apart from Richard's. There was so much chemistry she could have filled a high school's curriculum talking about it, and to dismiss it would have cheapened it.

'Yes, it's serious.'

'Oh.'

The coffee was awful—had always been awful when Richard had made it, come to think of it. She wasn't sure how he did it but he never got it right. Two sugars, the best instant coffee on the supermarket shelf and a generous splash of milk and it still didn't work. Just about summed them up really. Good-looking, good job, nice home, and still it hadn't worked out. Tipping it down the sink, the meaning was wasted on Richard.

'I'm going to have a shower and change, I'll be down in a moment.'

She needed a moment to compose herself and to get out of this ridiculous dress, but, stepping under the shower, she hated the water that doused her body, hating it for removing every lingering trace of Hugh. Wrapping a towel around her, she picked up her dress, inhaling the tangy citrus that was so much part of the man she loved as if gaining strength. She dressed for Richard, in the sloppiest leggings and most faded T-shirt, totally ignoring her make-up bag. Opening her bedside drawer, Rachael felt her bitterness vanish, a sting behind her eyes so alien it took a moment to register they were tears as she pulled out the simple box, adorned with shells and starfish filled with all her memories. She wondered, begged of herself just how she should play this.

It would be too much to walk in the lounge and place it on the coffee-table, expecting Richard to just open right up, but she didn't want to lose the moment by having to escape upstairs to retrieve it. On legs that felt like jelly, Rachael made her way downstairs, carefully placing the box by the phone, ready to retrieve it when the moment was right.

Was there a flicker of disappointment in Richard's eyes as she sat down on the sofa in front of him? Had he expected the groomed woman he had seen last night to appear again?

'Better?'

Rachael nodded. 'You said you weren't coping,' she started carefully.

'I'm not.' He looked around the lounge and out the window, his eyes finally coming back to her. 'Work's been hard.'

'I know.' She did know, Rachael knew only too well how hard it was to smile and just carry on.

'I've lost a couple of big clients.' He raked a hand through his hair. 'They expect you to come along to these functions, to say the right thing all the time, to look the part...' He was fiddling with his ring finger now, his empty ring finger. 'You've met Susie.'

Rachael frowned as she nodded, unsure where he was heading.

'It's just not working.'

'I'm sorry. She seemed...' Her voice trailed off. There was no polite way to describe Susie.

'She's not you,' Richard said, and the break in his voice filled the strained air. 'I should never have let you go.'

'We weren't happy, Richard,' she pointed out. 'We fought all the time.'

'But things could be better,' he argued. 'I really need you, Rachael. I know that now, and last night was the final straw. Even the other partners say I was mad to let you go.'

'What have the other partners got to do with anything?' Rachael said through paling lips. 'Where on earth do they come into this?'

'They don't,' Richard said in a voice that did nothing to convince her. 'This is about you and I, about getting back what we lost. I'm sure with a bit of give and take on both sides we could make things work.' His looked at her imploringly. 'You seem so much better now.'

'You mean thinner.' There was a warning note to her voice, which Richard quickly heeded.

'Not just thinner,' he said. 'Happier, back in the swing of things. Maybe now that you're over your depression we could give it another try.'

'My depression!' She stood up, her ears ringing with his choice of words. 'And where the hell were you when I was getting over my "depression"?' Her voice was rising with each and every word, every livid nerve in her body snapping in fury. 'Where were you when I needed you to be there for me, for both of us? At some bloody five-course dinner, making up ridiculous excuses to explain my absence when anyone with half a brain would have known why I didn't want to come out; anyone with an ounce of compassion would have known that I wasn't up to "networking". You should have been at home, Richard, not feeling sorry for yourself and wondering why I couldn't still fit into a size eight dress, wondering when I'd snap out of it and get on with being the perfect wife. You should have been at home.'

She sat down again, stunned at the venom in her attack, the violence of her words surprising even herself. 'What about Amy?' she whispered. 'What about our daughter?' Surely she couldn't have got it so wrong, surely Richard not coping wasn't to do with losing a couple of clients or the fact his fellow partners were moaning about his choice of date?

'If you want to have another baby,' Richard started nervously, still reeling from her outburst. 'If that's what it takes then that's what we'll do.'

'That's it?' Her voice was shaking, her eyes widening incredulously. 'That's your solution to our "little problem"?'

'Rachael, please, stop making me out to be the bad guy. All I wanted, all I ever wanted was the best for you.'

'The best for you, you mean.'

'There's no shame in looking nice, there's nothing wrong with taking a pride in your appearance. You think that hotshot plastic surgeon would look twice at you if you were overweight?'

'Yes,' she answered definitely, immediately. 'He cares for me, Richard—me, not for some trophy he can display to his colleagues, not as some asset that might help further his career. And I know as sure as I'm standing here that if we'd just lost a baby the last thing he'd even notice would be if my dress size had gone up.'

But Richard couldn't see it, simply refused to believe that what Rachael was saying might possibly be true.

'Then you're a fool, Rachael,' he said spitefully. 'And if that's your attitude then you're only going to get hurt again. Anyone can say the right things when the going's good. Anyone can make promises at the beginning of a relationship, say the right thing because it's what the other one wants to hear. I wonder if this—' his lips sneered around the name '—Hugh would be quite so understanding if he'd been through what I'd had to put up with.'

'Get out.' The tremor in her voice had doubled, her lips were white as she struggled to stay calm. 'Get out of my home, Richard.' Something in her eyes, her voice, her body told him that she meant business. 'And don't even think about coming back.'

'You're just going to be hurt,' was his parting shot as he pulled open the front door.

She saw it then, Amy's memory box, standing unopened on the hallway table, the final trigger as she watched him leave. Running up the hallway, there was so much Rachael wanted to scream at him, so much she wanted to say. She didn't care about the neighbours, didn't care about anything except righting a thousand wrongs, unleashing some of the anger that seemed to be suffocating her. But as she wrenched the door open huge arms held her, huge arms that wrapped around her like a vice, pushing her inside, holding her tight when she wanted to run, pulling her back as she crossed over the edge, burying his lips in her hair and gently hushing her as she fought like a cat to get past.

'He's gone, Rachael,' Hugh rasped. 'Just let him go.'

'I hate him,' she said. 'I hate him.' Burying her head in Hugh's chest, she breathed in that smell, too much, much too much, but everything that she needed right now. 'I thought you'd gone.'

'I'm here,' he whispered.

'I didn't think you'd come back.'

'I'm not just jealous.' He half smiled, pulling her gently back to look up at him. 'I'm obsessive as well. One drive round the block and I was back.'

He led her to the sofa. Pulling her down into his lap, he held her for a moment as she wrestled with the tears in her eyes.

'Let it out,' he said gently. 'I'm here.'

'He said we could have another baby.' An angry sob strangling her voice as she felt his grip tighten around her, heard the anger in the rapid breath he exhaled. But Hugh didn't say anything, just sat quietly holding her, letting her continue. 'I don't want another baby, I want…I want…'

But she couldn't say it, couldn't do it, couldn't quite let go of that part of herself. Closing her eyes, she took a deep breath, knowing that there was going to be nothing pretty about her tears, scared, so scared of what might be swept away when the floodgates finally opened, so deep her pain Rachael truly thought she might vomit, might scream like a banshee if she gave in now.

Yes, Hugh might love her, but there were some things he really didn't need to see...

'I'm fine now.'

How long they sat there she wasn't sure. Hugh held her, not saying a word, just holding her as the shadows on the wall lengthened and she stared dry-eyed at the darkening sky, only moving to grab a throw from the sofa when the cool change swept in. Wrapping it tightly around her, Hugh pulled her back into his arms, holding her tightly as if somehow his warmth might thaw the icy wall around that warm and vulnerable heart, wishing he could stroke away all that pain, say the right thing, but knowing deep down that words didn't always help.

Finally, when her eyes were heavy and sleep was the only escape, Rachael pulled away. 'I think I'll go to bed.' She answered the unspoken question that hung in the air. 'Alone.'

'Don't make me leave you, Rachael,' he pleaded.

'Please, Hugh, I really need to be alone.'

'No, you don't,' he argued. 'I want to be here with you.'

'Don't.' Her hand shot up to her ears and she closed her eyes. 'I just don't need this right now.'

She felt so washed out and so unsteady when she stood it was like she had been in bed for a week with the flu. 'You understand, don't you?' she asked as he reluctantly turned to go.

His hand stilled on the doorhandle. His back was

to her, but she heard the pain in his voice as he answered, 'Not really, Rachael, but I'm trying to.'

And as he quietly slipped away she stood in the dark living room, listening to the hum of his engine purring through the empty streets.

She needed to be alone, needed just a tiny breathing space to digest all that had happened. The only thing was, Rachael realised too late as she climbed the lonely stairs to bed, watching Hugh leave had been the hardest part of the day.

CHAPTER ELEVEN

'YOU wanted to see me?' Rachael grinned as she walked into the office and saw Helen calmly sitting with her feet up, eating a massive doughnut as she read a pamphlet on liposuction.

'Have you seen these pamphlets?' Helen asked, totally ignoring the question. 'They can do all sorts, you know. Apparently Dr Fielding is one of the best at liposuction—they just suck all the fat away and once it's gone it doesn't come back.'

'Rubbish,' Rachael scoffed. 'Nothing's that easy. So what did you want me for?'

'You know how we've got a few empty beds? Well, the nurse co-ordinator found out and she wants an RN to go and help in Outpatients.' She watched as Rachael pulled an unpleasant face. 'To help with the Dr Connell's clinic,' she added with a satisfied smile as Rachael face instantly perked up. 'Can I say that you'll do it? It's just blood pressures and a few dressing changes.'

'Sure. Oh, and, Helen, you know we've got that overseas patient coming in this afternoon?'

'Kimbi?'

'That's the one. Can I be allocated to look after her? It's not for that,' she said quickly as Helen gave a wink. 'Hugh was talking about her at the fund-raiser and it sounds really interesting. I'd love to nurse her.'

'Deal.' Helen laughed. 'If you could see your

face. You always frown when you're telling fib, it's a dead give-away.'

'I'm useless at lying,' Rachael mumbled. 'Still, I really am interested.'

'You can get rid of all those lines, you know,' Helen started, but Rachael gave a dismissive flick of her hand.

'I just spent yesterday with Richard. I don't need a lecture from you,' she warned.

'Well, look at this, then.' Helen rummaged through the piles of brochures. 'Botox injections, you can have them done in your lunch-break.' Curiosity got the better of Rachael and she picked up a leaflet, pulling her face into curious angles as she felt the frown lines on her brow.

'It takes ten years off. I'm getting it done.'

'Your not serious.' Rachael laughed.

'Absolutely. Four children, five if you include Jack, plus full-time nursing—I reckon I deserve a treat.'

Hugh, of course, had to walk in as Helen and Rachael were peering into hand mirrors, pulling their faces into all sorts of weird expressions.

'Did the co-ordinator tell you I needed a nurse?'

'They did.' Helen beamed, not remotely embarrassed. 'And here she is. Hugh, you're not interested in hosting my party, are you?' She gave a quick wink to Rachael to show she was joking. 'Apparently Botox has taken over Tupperware, I'm thinking of throwing a party.'

'Well, don't invite any nurses from Theatre,' Hugh uncharacteristically snapped. 'An impassive face above a mask might be the difference between a right and left hip being fixed. We rely on those little frowns down there.

'Anyway,' he added impatiently, gesturing to Rachael to follow him as he picked up a pile of files, 'you'll have to get Dr Fielding. In case you hadn't noticed, I don't do Botox injections.'

Rachael almost had to run to keep up with him as he marched smartly down the corridor. She knew he was upset, knew he was a bit bruised and put out, but perhaps more pointedly Rachael understood why. They had made love, wonderful breathtaking love, over and over, and then Richard had turned up. Hugh had said and done all the right things—come back, held her, loved her—and she had dismissed him.

No wonder he wasn't at his sunniest.

But that night alone had done wonders for her, given her the chance to think, really think things through. It was over with Richard.

It was Hugh she loved and she didn't care who knew it.

Rachael was also rather too painfully aware that for the most part he had seen only the darker side of her. Fun she could be, flirty too if that was what it took to get a smile on his face.

Hugh deserved a break.

Mind you, there was only so much *fun* to be had in an outpatients clinic, and as for flirting, forget it. If she had thought cosmetic surgery was glamorous, one morning spent with tragically scarred people soon put paid to that. Hugh worked like a trojan and Rachael fared not much better.

'That's about it,' he said eventually, snapping his lid on his pen. 'Thanks for your help.'

'My pleasure.' Rachael beamed. 'Look, Hugh, about last night, thanks for being there.'

'I wasn't there,' he pointed out. 'You asked me to leave.'

'I meant before that.' Rachael said quickly. 'I've been doing some thinking, a lot of thinking actually, and I was wrong to ask you to leave last night. I only really realised it after you'd left.' Her words seemed to mollify him slightly and she let out a sigh of relief as he placed the pen back on his desk. 'I haven't blown it, have I? I mean, you're not so sick of me and my dramas you're about to turn tail and run?'

'All this time,' he said slowly, 'I've been so worried about you, Rachael. Trying to work out how to make things easier for you, trying to be sure that I don't hurt you further.' He let out a long ragged breath. 'Maybe I'm the one who's going to end up hurt.'

'It's over with Richard,' she said firmly. 'It always has been. I only let him in yesterday because of—'

'Amy.'

She nodded.

'Another thing that's out of bounds.'

'What do you mean?'

'You won't let me in, Rachael,' Hugh said wearily, the pain evident in his voice. 'I know it might be too soon and maybe I'm expecting too much, but I know how I feel, Rachael, I've known more or less since the day I met you. And I can't just have half of you. I don't want to be sent away again. I want to be there with you, for the bad times as well as the good. It's up to you,' he finished. 'I can't do this by halves.'

He stood up to go and Rachael simply couldn't bear it, didn't want the morning to end on that note.

'Don't go,' she called.

'It's lunchtime, I'm hungry.'

'I grabbed these in my coffee-break.' She held up two Cellophane-wrapped sandwiches at which Hugh promptly turned up his nose.

'I'm going to the doctors' mess to eat.'

'Who's the one walking off now?' Hugh stopped walking but Rachael still sensed his reluctance to stay. 'I hear what you're saying, Hugh, and I really do understand, but can we just leave it for a while? Can we just enjoy our lunch?'

'Enjoy lunch?' he said, his lips twitching at the edges. 'What's that going to solve?'

'Nothing probably,' she said brightly. 'Except for the fact that I like being with you.'

She had definitely hit the mark because those gorgeous lips spread into a reluctant smile and Rachael moved quickly, determined they would have this brief lunch together.

'Show me how this works,' she said quickly, gesturing, partly for something to say and also because for the entire morning it had fascinated her.

'It's just a simulator.'

'So show me how it works.'

With a sigh he sat down, clicking with the mouse until his face appeared on the screen. 'I use it to show patients how they might look after surgery.' He fiddled more with the mouse, shaving an inch off his jaw line, snubbing the end of his nose. 'Have a go if you like.'

Nervously she took the mouse, staring at his image on the screen as he guided her around the toolbox. 'Off you go,' he said lightly.

But she couldn't do it. His face was so perfect, so absolutely right it would be like taking a hammer to the statue of David. She made a couple of pathetic attempts at his nose and amputated his eyelids. By the time she had finished he looked like the potatoman toy her nephew played with.

'Do me,' she said quickly as he went to pick up his pager.

'I'm in a rush.'

'Come on,' she pleaded in what she hoped was a sort of happy, flirty voice, anything to end the morning on a lighter note. Slipping onto the stool in front of the camera, she waited as he clicked away.

'OK, you're up,' Hugh said. His voice was thick, his breathing slightly ragged as she leant over his shoulder.

'Go on, then,' Rachael urged. 'Transform me.'

'What do you want me to do?'

'Come off it, Hugh, what do you think I want you to do? Get rid of it.'

'Rid of what?'

'This.' She tapped impatiently at her cheek. 'This damned mole. Don't try and pretend you haven't noticed it.'

'Of course I've noticed it. I happen to like it.'

'Sure,' Rachael muttered, watching as he dragged the mouse over her left cheek. 'Go on,' she urged, wondering why on earth he was taking so long. She had been watching him all morning, clicking away with lightning speed, and yet he was taking an age to remove a tiny mole.

'There,' he said finally, leaning back in his chair. 'Happy now?'

'I don't know,' she said slowly, staring incredulously at her image. In the scheme of things it was such a tiny blemish, such a small thing, yet this mole had been the bane of her life. What had felt like merciless teasing—'What's on your face, Rachael?'—still rang in her ears from the second form, and her clumsy attempts to cover the thing with concealer weren't a particularly distant memory. Even though Richard's timing had been appalling, having it removed wasn't something she hadn't already considered. So here she was.

Moleless or whatever the technical term was.

'Can you do it? I mean, will you take it off for me?'

'Before or after the Botox injections?'

'That was a joke.' Rachael laughed but it died on her lips when she saw the look on his face. 'Hugh, it was a joke,' she insisted.

'For someone who's so opposed to cosmetic surgery, you seem terribly interested all of a sudden.'

'I'm just looking at your machine. Heavens, I'm surrounded by it every day at work, it would be neglectful of me not to be interested.'

'So it has nothing to do with the fact your ex-husband's back on the scene, this sudden desire for eternal youth.'

'If you'd known me in my teenage years,' Rachael retorted smartly, 'then you'd know I've absolutely no desire to relive them. I had a face full of spots and braces you could wire a house with, and, no, this has absolutely nothing to do with Richard. This is to do with me.'

'Well, I won't do it.'

'I'm not after a freebie,' she retorted nastily.

'It wouldn't be appropriate,' he bit back in an almost prim voice.

'It's a tiny mole, for heaven's sake,' Rachael argued, wondering just where this row had flown in from, wondering how it had all gone so horribly wrong and utterly determined not to back down. 'I'm not asking for a face lift.'

'We're involved, Rachael. Ethically speaking, it wouldn't be right for me to operate on you.'

'If we're so involved, Hugh, why are you picking up your stethoscope? Why are you heading off to the doctors' mess instead of sharing you lunch with me?' She took a deep breath, anger blurring her senses, hurt that he was leaving and determined to hit back. 'Do you know what I think?'

'No,' he muttered. 'But I'm sure you're about to tell me.'

'I think you only like me when I'm down.' She watched as he turned, knew she was way out of line with her spiteful words but she couldn't stop herself. It was the sort of row that should only be had in a bedroom, preferably when there was no means of escape, no car in the drive or pager that could go off, when silly spiteful things could be taken back in the fullness of time, or put right in bed, but she was too angry to acknowledge the warning bells that were alarming in her head.

'Don't I cry enough for you, Hugh? It seems to me that the second I assert myself or actually look like I'm enjoying myself, you don't like it. Do you like your women emotionally needy, Hugh?'

'That's the most vile thing you could have said.'

His lips were white and a muscle pounded in his cheek. 'I'll tell you how I like my women, Rachael, warm and loving and tender, not hankering over their ex-husband, not pushing me away when I try to get close. I'm going to the doctors' mess, and before you accuse me of walking away I'll tell you why I'm going. For one thing, the food's better.' He tossed the sandwich into a wastepaper basket before turning smartly on his heel. 'And, frankly, so is the company.'

CHAPTER TWELVE

KIMBI was gorgeous.

One look at those velvety brown eyes and that slow, shy smile and Rachael knew why Hugh's voice had wavered slightly when he had spoken about her. If ever there was a patient to put Rachael's troubles into perspective, Kimbi was the one.

Through the words of the translator Rachael learned of her horrific injuries, the twelve operations she had endured in the past two years, heard from her mother how grateful they were for the chance for their daughter to live a normal life.

'She likes to dance,' Jelai the translator said with a smile. 'And she tells me that now she talks the most in her class. She makes up for lost time,' Jelai said with a small note of triumph.

'Wonderful.' Rachael smiled. 'Could you tell her that I'm just going to take her blood pressure and temperature and then I'll page Dr Connell and let him know that she's here.'

At just the mention of Hugh's name Kimbi, her mother and the translator seemed to brighten.

Rachael, too.

She longed to see him, longed for the chance to apologise, but not here. Later, tonight, she would try and take back the things she had said, give him a chance to explain his sudden change of mood.

Pulling up Kimbi's gown, Rachael frowned

slightly. Unfortunately, it didn't go unnoticed by Jelai and the thought of those wretched Botox injections suddenly seemed like a good idea.

'Is everything all right?' Jelai was watching her like a hawk.

'Kimbi has a rather large bruise on her arm.'

A couple of minutes' talk was translated back into one short sentence. 'She banged her arm, carrying water.'

Rachael nodded but she felt far from reassured. The bruise was dark, large and the fact it seemed to have gone relatively unnoticed bothered her. Popping the tympanic thermometer into Kimbi's ear, the reading was delivered in less than a second. This time Rachael kept a check on her features, deliberately not commenting when she saw the low-grade temperature reading.

'Apart from the bruise, has Kimbi been well recently?'

Another prolonged conversation took place as Rachael sat on the edge of the bed, listening to the musical language.

'She has a sore throat.'

'I see.' Gently she pulled down Kimbi's lower eyelids, noticing the pallor not so readily visible in someone with darker skin.

'Right, I'll just give Dr Connell a page. Can I get you ladies anything—a drink or some sandwiches? Kimbi's not scheduled for Theatre until tomorrow so she can eat as well.'

She didn't get up to go, knowing the simple question would take a moment to answer.

More than a moment actually. Kimbi rummaged in her locker, pulling out menus as a rather elaborate conversation took place with a lot of hand waving. The translation when it came was strangely disappointing.

'No, thank you. We are all just fine.'

'The call bell's here.' Placing it on the table in front of her patient, Rachael took a moment to go explain the rather complicated device, realising that when Kimbi had last been here she had been on the old ward.

'Lights, television, nurse call bell,' she said, as Kimbi practised pressing all three, the television springing into life, the lights blazing on around them as Rachael's little orange pager duly sprang into life. 'You've got it.'

'Sister,' Jelai called her as she went to go. 'Dr Connell shares a pizza with us tonight. Please, can we cancel Kimbi's dinner order? It would be shameful to waste the food.'

'Certainly.' Well, there went her cosy dinner and chance to apologise. It looked like Hugh was booked up.

Hugh was in Theatre, of course, and it took an age for him to answer. His words were curt and Rachael knew it had nothing to do with keeping it short for the sake of the theatre sister's arm.

'Tell her I'll be along after my list.'

'She's ordering pizza for you.'

He didn't even grace her with a small laugh.

'Hugh…'

Even though he was two floors up and a long corridor away, she felt him tense. 'Not now, Rachael.'

'It's not about us.' Rachael swallowed, utterly unable to resist fishing a little. 'Assuming, of course, that there is an us?' Again no answer, no clue as to what he was thinking. 'It's about Kimbi.'

'What about her?'

'She's got a low-grade temp and a sore throat, and Hugh, she looks ever so pale.'

'She's probably got a cold, and egg and steaks aren't exactly a regular dish where she's from.'

'She's *very* pale,' Rachael insisted.

'She always is. Normally I get the dietician to take a look at her. She'll probably need some food supplements while she's here.'

'There's a large bruise on her arm.'

She heard his pause, felt him tense again, but when his voice came it was light and easy. 'She lives a hard life, Rachael. I'll take a look when I'm up there—it will be nothing.'

'Hugh…' She waited for a response and when it didn't come she said it anyway. 'I'm sorry.'

She heard him mumble to the theatre sister, heard the click of the telephone hanging up, and standing for a moment holding the purring receiver, Rachel whispered the words again. 'I'm sorry, Hugh.'

Because she wanted to hang around, because she wanted to finish late and get a chance to see Hugh, of course the ward was quiet. So quiet, in fact, that the late staff took an early coffee-break, coming back bang on three-thirty, which meant the early shift had the 'treat' of going home early.

Not that it would have made any difference. One glance at Hugh's theatre list and Rachael knew that Kimbi wouldn't be getting her pizza much before eight tonight.

'What are you dawdling for?' Helen's cheerful

voice behind her made her jump. 'Do you want to hold my hand?'

'Sorry?' Rachael gave her friend a rather startled look, and then, despite her pensive mood, Rachael's face broke into a grin. 'People might start talking.'

'I meant at Outpatients. I'm going to book in with Dr Fielding for those injections.'

'You're serious, aren't you?'

'Deadly. I deserve a treat. You're looking at the new me, Rachael. I'm going to start putting on make-up and I'm going to spend some of my savings on me for once instead of on designer clothes for the kids. I've decided that I'm going to grow old disgracefully.'

'You're fine just as you are,' Rachael insisted.

'I know.' Helen shrugged as she walked. 'But I'm sick of being fine. I want to be great. It's all right,' she added as she looked at Rachael's worried face. 'I'm not booking in for liposuction or a boob job. I just want to feel a bit better about myself. There's nothing wrong with that.'

There wasn't, Rachael realised. Hugh had been right. She did have some prejudices but they were slowly being eroded. Richard was an extreme but there was a middle ground, and a vast one at that. There was a huge difference between vanity and self-pride.

'I'm going to get this mole off.'

'Rachael!'

'Don't look so alarmed. This has nothing to do with Richard, this is all about me. I've always hated it. *Hated* it,' she added firmly. 'And you're right—there's nothing wrong with wanting to feel good about yourself. We'll be gorgeous together.'

Linking arms, they laughed as they made their way to the plastics secretary's desk, trying not to be overwhelmed as a clone of Susie tapped away on her computer.

'What can I do for you ladies?'

Helen was the bravest and spoke first. 'I want to make an appointment with Dr Fielding.'

'Fine. For what?'

Helen hesitated. It was one thing plucking up the courage to see a doctor, but another thing entirely telling the whole waiting room what you were having done.

'I need to know,' 'Susie' said, 'so that I can book you in on the right day. Dr Fielding does a lot of different procedures.'

'Botox,' Helen mumbled. At least, Rachael assumed she'd said Botox—it had sounded more like a low grumble out of the corner of her mouth.

'Fine.' A pussycat smile and a stroke of manicured fingers and Helen had recited her name and was the proud owner of a pink business card with an appointment date.

'Did you want anything, Miss…?'

'Holroyd.' It was Rachael mumbling now. 'I wanted to see him about getting this…' she tapped her cheek '…this mole removed.'

'Excuse me one moment.' 'Susie's' very pert little bottom swung on her stool and Rachael watched with growing indignation as that pussycat smile widened. 'Dr Connell, I thought you were in theatre?'

'Between patients,' he growled with just the briefest of nods to Helen and Rachael. 'Can I see my diary? One of my patients just called. She needs to come in to Outpatients urgently, so I've pencilled her in for seven p.m. Can you pull out the notes for me?'

'You could have rung for that,' 'Susie' purred, as Rachael thought the same thing. Maybe he was more interested in the groomed Susies than he made out.

'Not for this, though,' Hugh replied. Grabbing a prescription chart, he started to write. 'Tell the outpatients sister to apply the local anaesthetic gel before she pages me. It will give it a chance to start working.' He was tapping on the computer, his broad shoulders the only view of him as he located the patient's hospital number and details for the prescription chart, effectively dismissing the three of them.

'Sorry about that. Now...' The secretary shuffled a sheaf of papers together. 'You wanted that mole taken off.'

Rachael was saved from a reply, saved from anything actually, as a prescription chart was angrily tossed across the desk. 'I'll be in Theatre,' Hugh growled. Stalking off without a further word, the three women were left in an invisible cloud of aftershave as they gathered their individual thoughts.

'Nothing for a month.' 'Susie' smiled. 'He's fully booked. However...' lowering her voice, she leant forward just enough to give Rachael a rather too good view of her beautifully tanned cleavage. 'I know I shouldn't be saying this.' She looked at the two name badges. 'But with you both being staff and everything, I'm sure it doesn't matter: Dr Connell, he's the one who was just here, does the most beautiful work. He's done a few bits for me in his time.' She gave a girly giggle as Rachael stood there, fuming. 'Would you like me to see if he can squeeze you in? He's got a couple of cancellations next week.'

'Better not.' Rachael's smile was far from sweet. 'I've already discussed it with *Hugh* and, given the fact that we're involved, he didn't feel it would be appropriate for him to perform surgery on me.'

'What have I done?' she groaned to Helen a little later as they walked away, clutching their referral cards.

'Doesn't mean you have to follow it through,' Helen said comfortingly. 'It's only an appointment. You can always back out at the last minute.'

'I wasn't talking about my mole,' Rachael snapped, unable to believe that Helen didn't see the problem! 'I might as well have taken out a full-page ad that Hugh and I are on together.'

Helen didn't bat an eyelid. 'It's hardly a state secret. Most of the ward knows anyway. Trevor's like a girl, the way he gossips.' She gave a shrug. 'You know what this place is like. It will be around the whole hospital in a matter of days anyway, you just gave it a bit of a nudge.'

'The only trouble is...' Rachael closed her eyes and sank back against the wall '...I don't know whether or not we are involved. I think I've really blown it.'

Helen was wonderful. The school run and four children wanting a quick dinner before footy training was organised with a few quick calls into her brick-sized ancient mobile phone, and before she knew it Rachael was sitting in a bar, clutching a large glass of wine, with the sympathetic face of her friend on the other side of the table, listening as she told her sorry tale.

'I said the most terrible things,' Rachael said for the hundredth time.

'Yes, you did.' Helen was driving so her vice was a huge slab of mud cake with thickened cream running rivers down the warm chocolate. 'But that's what happens when people argue.'

'But to accuse him of only wanting me when I'm down—'

'Must have hurt,' Helen interrupted. 'Look, Rachael, what do you want from a relationship? What's the most important thing?' she gave a cheeky grin. 'Apart from sex.'

'Respect,' Rachael said thoughtfully. 'Trust, acceptance.'

Helen shook her head. 'Honesty. If you're truly honest with each other, all the rest follow. Richard wasn't honest with you. He wanted the trophy wife, the flash car and the wonderful career, and he pretended he was doing it for you both when the truth was he was doing it for himself. Hugh is being honest. He knows what you've been through, knows that you're not being honest with him, and perhaps more to the point he knows that when you say everything's fine, you're not being honest with yourself either.'

'I can't just turn it on like a tap. I can't just start crying because it's expected of me.'

'No one's asking you to, but you do need to talk about Amy.'

'I do.' Rachael shook her head, irritated. She had come here to talk about Hugh, for the hope of some insight, not a full-blown grief counselling session.

'How many times a day do I talk about the boys? She's your daughter, you're allowed to talk about her, it's too soon to be putting it behind you. It's not even a year yet.'

'Tomorrow,' Rachael said quietly, and Helen's cake froze midway to her mouth. 'It will be a year tomorrow.'

She knew Helen was waiting for her to elaborate, waiting for more, but she simply couldn't give it. Thankfully Helen didn't push, taking her time instead to finish her cake.

'He's jealous.'

'No, he isn't,' Rachael said. 'And if he is, there's no need. I've told him it's all over between Richard and me.'

'Well, I suggest you tell him again. And if he doesn't listen, tell him once more.'

'He should trust me.'

'Why? How did you feel when that receptionist was acting all proprietorial?'

'Jealous,' Rachael mumbled. 'Angry.'

'With no good reason. Hugh did nothing to indicate they were an item but it still didn't stop you showing your cards, stamping your mark on him.'

'Don't.' Rachael cringed at the memory.

'I'd say Hugh's got more reason to be jealous. Tell him why you're getting this mole off, tell him again that it has nothing to do with Richard and everything to do with you.' She stood up, picking up her bag as they split the bill and wandered out into the street. 'Once you get past this, once you can both be honest with each other, the rest will follow. Come on, I'll drive you home.'

'Helen…' They were sitting in the car with a pile

of footballs and hockey sticks vying for space on the back seat. 'Don't get the injections. You really are great just as you are.'

Laughing, Helen turned on the engine. 'Forget it. I'm not the one on the guilt trip, so you've no chance of talking me out of it. Come Tuesday, Rachael, I'm there.'

CHAPTER THIRTEEN

RACHAEL, queen of repair jobs.

She looked great, well, not great perhaps but completely normal. Just another late shift and another nurse rushing to get there on time. No one could ever have guessed the pain behind her smile, no one could have known as she burst through the ward doors in a cloud of perfume and newly washed hair that this was the second most difficult day of her life.

The first didn't bear thinking about.

Hugh was there in his office, tapping away on his computer just as he had been the night she'd met him, only now there was so much more between them. So much more that, glancing at her watch, Rachael knew she couldn't just walk past.

'Hugh.' He didn't look up but his fingers paused over the keyboard. 'I paged you last night. You didn't answer.'

'I meant to. I just got caught up. It was gone midnight by the time I got out of here.'

'I just wanted to explain something.' He wasn't making this easy. The back of his head wasn't the most expressive part of his body but Rachael battled on anyway.

'What I said yesterday was unforgivable.' She gave a tiny, nervous laugh. 'Hopefully not that unforgivable, though.' When he didn't move she carried on tentatively, 'I'm so sorry, Hugh, and about

170

my mole. I'm not getting it taken off because of Richard. It's because of me, Hugh. I just want to do this. I've always wanted to do it. I guess it's a bit of fresh start—out with the old, in with the new.' She was rambling now but his silence gave her no choice. 'I've always hated it—'

'Will you just shut up about your stupid mole?' He swung round, his green eyes blazing, utter contempt on his face, and Rachael jumped back as if she'd been shot. 'The morning I'm having and you waltz in here with your narcissistic reasons for having your mole off...' He took a deep breath then pressed his balled hands to his forehead as Rachael stood there, stunned. 'Rachael, I'm sorry,' he rasped. 'I'm sorry,' he said again. 'I just don't need to hear this right now.'

Her lips were white, her eyes wide, at his outburst. 'Fine.' She pulled open the door, tossing her hair as she turned on her heel. 'Sorry I disturbed you.'

'Rachael...' He called out her name but she didn't go back. She could hear the need, the note of anxiety in his voice as he called her but, like Hugh, she didn't need to hear it right now.

Today of all days.

The mood was equally volatile at handover. Helen's face looked like a thundercloud, so far removed from her usually sunny disposition that Rachael didn't even bother with small talk, just took her seat in the spare chair as Trevor came in to give handover.

'Who'd got Orange Bay?' he asked first, and as Rachael went to answer Helen beat her too it.

'I'll take it.'

'I've been in there all week,' Rachael piped up. 'I wanted to stay in there.'

Helen gave a shrug. 'Wait till you hear handover.'

Trevor stared at his sheet for a moment, not one little joke, not one light-hearted comment. 'Side ward, Orange Bay,' he started. 'Kimbi Adoussi, ten-year-old female, overseas visitor. In for grafting to her left cheek and division of scar tissue. Hugh came last night to admit her, he took some blood work.' Rachael could feel herself frowning. The detail he was going into about a routine pre-admission was lengthy and the ominous feeling that had visited yesterday, the one Hugh had dismissed, had reassured her was nothing, was creeping back. She looked at Helen's strained face, looked over at Trevor, for once sounding professional. 'Her blood work came back this morning. It will need to be confirmed by a bone marrow biopsy, but the upshot is it's pretty definite that she's got leukaemia.' He sat quietly for a moment, waiting for the collective gasp to fade, allowing the terrible news to sink in, and, Rachael realised, struggled to compose himself. 'Dr Connell has spent the last couple of hours on the telephone to the Children's Hospital. There's a bed for her on the oncology ward, the ambulance has been booked, she'll need a nurse escort.'

'I've told the co-ordinator to organise one,' Helen broke in.

'I'll go.' Rachael's voice was quiet but definite. 'I admitted her yesterday. It will be better for Kimbi.'

'But not for you,' Helen said gently as the whole room turned to Rachael. 'Today of all days.'

'I'll do it,' Rachael said, more loudly this time, and Helen gave a reluctant nod. 'Has she been told?'

Trevor cleared his throat. 'Hugh just spoke to her, to her mother, too. It wasn't very easy, with the translator and everything. He's pretty upset,' he added. 'He's just locked himself away in the doctors' room. I'd leave him be if I were you. I don't think he wants company right now.'

A moan escaped Rachael's lips as she realised what she had done. His 'narcissistic' comment, which had hurt so much, seemed pretty much merited, given what she now knew.

'He wants to be told when the ambulance gets here, though.' Trevor broke into her thoughts. 'He wants to say goodbye to Kimbi, though if I know Hugh he'll be heading off there tonight for another pizza.' He looked up as the door opened and the familiar green outfit of the paramedics came into view. 'That was quick.'

'The doctor said it was high priority.'

Helen stood up at the same time as Rachael. 'You're sure about this?'

'I'm sure.'

'OK, I'll come and say goodbye. Trevor, you carry on with handover, I'll catch up later.'

Kimbi looked so much more fragile than yesterday. The happy, laughing eyes were now clouded with fear and she clung to her mother's hand as the paramedics gently lifted her onto the stretcher. The translator's voice was loud and seemed to add to the confusion, but Rachael knew it was necessary.

'Tell Kimbi I'm just going to get Dr Connell.'

'No need.' He was standing at the door, smiling, only the tiniest muscle flicking in his cheek belying his cheerful stance. 'Hey, Kimbi, leaving so soon? Who's going to be my pizza buddy now?'

The answer took ages but a shy smile came to Kimbi's lips as Jelai relayed her words. 'You. She wants you to come and see her at the new hospital.' Jelai's dark eyes flicked back to Kimbi who spoke in a soft, anxious voice. 'Are they as nice there?'

Hugh came over. Taking her little hand in his, he paused for a moment before answering. 'They're very, very nice there, Kimbi, and very clever. And they're going to look after you beautifully. And when you're better you're going to come right back here and we'll finish what we started, OK? And as for coming to see you, you've got yourself a date.'

A little giggle at the end of the translation told Rachael Kimbi had got the message. 'Time to go,' Rachael said as brightly as she could. Picking up the notes, she unnecessarily tucked the blanket a bit tighter around her small charge because, unfortunately, that was all she could do for Kimbi.

That and keep on smiling.

Ambulances had always fascinated Rachael, even as a child. Maybe they had sown those first seeds that would see her go into nursing. There was something about those tinted windows, the knowledge that behind them there was a hive of activity going on, someone in there perhaps desperately ill, a person needing help. And today, as they battled with the city traffic, as she held Kimbi's mother's hand and watched the trams clattering past, as they turned into the hospital, she wondered if anyone looking in could guess at the tragedy behind the windows. It took every ounce of professionalism she could muster to smile and make small talk as they made their journey.

Hugh had been right. The staff were nice. Very nice. And just what Kimbi needed now. But how they did it Rachael could only wonder. How could you work on a children's oncology ward with a fluffy toy around your neck and a bright smile on your face as you took the handover and still know instinctively how to put your patient at ease? She watched in awe as a nurse chatted easily with the translator, squeezing Kimbi's hand and winking as if they were old friends.

Kimbi was in the right place.

'We're going to grab a coffee.' Bill, one of the paramedics tapped her on the shoulder. 'Take your time, Rachael.'

So she did. She fussed about the little girl and saw her into bed, gave her handover to the nurse who knew more than her anyway and then it was time to say goodbye. She wasn't Hugh, she didn't have a big place in this little girl's life, so this was the hard part, saying goodbye to a patient that touched you more than most, remembering you were just the nurse.

'Sister…' Jelai caught up with her in the corridor, Kimbi's mum following anxiously behind. 'Kimbi's mother wishes you to pass something on.'

Rachael nodded, and because Kimbi wasn't there she matched their sombre faces and didn't pretend to smile.

'Dr Connell, when he told us, he kept saying sorry.'

'He was upset.' Rachael's voice was a croak.

'We know. He has been more than a doctor, he

is a very special friend.' She turned and spoke to Kimbi's mother and Rachael's heart went out to the woman as she heard her tired voice, watched the tears she hadn't cried in front of her daughter course down her cheeks. 'She says she has memories now, good ones, thanks to Dr Connell. He has nothing to be sorry for. Will you tell him that, please?'

'Of course.'

The ambulance ride back was subdued. the paramedics seemed to know she wasn't in the mood for a chat and Rachael sat in the back, glad of the darkened windows, looking out on a world that couldn't look in. As the back doors opened when they arrived at their own hospital, she accepted a hand and stepped down, blinking in the late afternoon sun. Standing in the ambulance bay, she watched as the world carried right on.

'How was she?'

Rachael had known Hugh would be waiting, had half expected to see him. 'She's in the right place,' Rachael said softly, her hand instinctively reaching for his arm.

'What I said before...'

'I deserved. Well, not really.' Rachael gave a slow smile. 'But given the circumstances.'

He was smiling now, but it was a glassy smile that she knew meant there had been tears. 'You always have to have the last word.'

'Always.' Fishing in her pocket, she pulled out her appointment card and ripped it up. 'The mole stays.'

'You do what's right for you.'

'I will,' she agreed. 'And it's staying. Today kind of puts things into perspective, doesn't it?'

She had said the wrong thing! Watching in horror, she saw his beautifully strong face crumple, saw the chasm of his pain.

'Hugh, this isn't your fault.'

'I know,' he rasped, 'but all I've put her through, all that pain, and for what? So that she looks the part, fits in. She's been to hell and back. That kid's had twelve operations and now this, all in the name of charity!'

'There's something they wanted me to tell you.'

His eyes narrowed and Rachael shook her head. 'Not here.'

They went inside, into the emergency department, and she pushed open a door, flicking the 'Engaged' sign on the interview-room door she sat down.

'This bit's from me,' she warned. 'Not her mother. If Kimbi hadn't been here, hadn't been having an operation, her leukaemia would have gone undiagnosed. Even if it had been picked up, what chance would she have had?' Her jumbled thoughts, which had taken shape in the ambulance, came together now. 'Here she's got some of the best medical brains in the world, a legion of skilled staff that will do their best for her.' She paused, struggling with a lump in her throat, with the sharp sting of a tear, which she blinked rapidly away. This was about Hugh, not her.

'Her mother wants to thank you.' She ignored his low, cynical rasp and carried on. 'For giving her good memories. You say it was for nothing. Well, that little girl got to eat and to dance and to go to school, and those are the things Kimbi and her mum will remember, not the pain of the surgery.'

Her words seemed to reach him, seemed to comfort him, and as he looked up he held his breath. Coursing down Rachael's cheeks were tears, real tears, and there was nothing subtle about them. His first instinct was to rush over, to put his arms around her, to beg her to stop, to quieten her. But a deeper instinct told him to wait.

'Memories matter,' she said, her voice dissolving to a strangled whisper as her buried grief came surging forth. 'I'd give anything for just one.'

Rachael screamed, an awful guttural scream that seemed to go on for ever. But because it was the emergency department, because tragedy darkened these doors every single day, no one popped their head in to see what the problem was, no one really noticed.

Except Hugh.

He held her and he rocked her and he held her some more as she cried for all she had lost. And when she thought she'd never stop, when the tears that racked her just kept on coming, he held her some more, his own tears blending with hers, and they cried together. For all she had been through, for all she had lost, and for all Amy could have, should have, would have been.

And later, much later, when a whole box of tissues lay in a crumpled heap, Rachael did what Hugh had predicted, what she had thought she never would.

She stopped.

And Hugh was still there.

'Better?'

'I don't know.'

'You will be,' he promised. 'Because I'm going

to make sure of it. We're going to get through this, Rachael, together.'

'I do feel better,' she gulped, taking the cup of water he had poured from the cooler, embarrassed and shy and utterly unable to meet his eyes. 'I must look a sight.'

'Terrible, actually.' He stood there for a moment just looking at her, love blazing from his eyes. 'But you're beautiful to me. Rachael, I can't do this for you. If I could, I'd take your pain. Forget halving it, sharing it, I'd take it all. But I can't.'

'I know.'

'You need to talk to someone, someone who's been through it, someone who understands.'

'I know,' she said again. 'And I will. I've got a number, I'll ring them tomorrow.'

'Today,' he said firmly. 'Today's Amy's birthday and you're going to mark it with something. And I'll be waiting right outside the door.' He smiled. 'Or in the car again if that's how you want it. But I'll be there, waiting.'

The tissues were finished and she fished in her bag for a handkerchief, nodding her thanks when Hugh handed her one. 'That's two you owe me.'

Rachael nodded. 'I owe you an apology as well.'

'You don't.' Hugh sighed. 'Let's just wipe the slate clean, huh? Let's just start again.'

'It's not that easy.' She swallowed. 'There's something else I need to tell you.' She was fiddling with the water cup, anything rather than look at him. 'I think I might have made things a bit difficult for you with your colleagues.'

'If you're about to confess your little confrontation with Enid—' she missed the humour behind his dry voice '—then don't worry about it. She's already told the whole hospital.'

'Enid?' swollen reddened eyes looked up for the first time. 'Who's Enid?'

'My receptionist.'

'She doesn't look like an Enid.'

'She doesn't, does she?' Hugh said with a smile. 'Neither does she look like a happily married mother of three on the wrong side of forty. A fine testimony to my surgical skills, I like to think.'

'Another thing I got wrong,' Rachael mumbled, scuffing the worn carpet with her foot.

'Oh, I don't know about that. You gave Enid the impression we were very much involved, so much so that if I'm not mistaken there's a brown envelope going around with our names on it right now.'

'A brown envelope?' Rachael gasped, 'but they're for babies and weddings and engagements and things. I only said we were involved.'

He came back to her then sat down and then pulled her onto his lap. 'Oh, we're involved all right, up to our necks if you ask me. And what with me being such a nice doctor and all, no doubt that envelope's filling pretty quickly.' He held her closer and she melted into him, holding her breath, not wanting to miss a single one of the delicious words that were coming. 'It would be a shame to waste it.' He kissed the top of her head, kissed her nose and then worked his way down to her swollen, chewed lips. 'Time for another name change if you think you're ready?'

'Oh, I'm ready,' Rachael sighed. 'I hate to sound narcissistic, but Connell sounds so much better than Holroyd.'

EPILOGUE

EVERY birth is special.

Every child is precious.

But if the theatre staff were a bit more tense, if the midwives a bit more efficient this morning, no one was apologising. This baby was extra-special and everyone who had read Rachael's notes knew it.

'Can you feel anything?' Dr Carmody was testing to see if the epidural had taken effect, making sure her abdomen was completely numb before he started the Caesarean section.

Rachael shook her head, lying back on the green pillow as Hugh rested his cheek against hers.

'Ready to meet this baby of yours?'

She couldn't speak but Hugh answered for her. 'We're ready.' His hand tightened on hers and she closed her eyes.

'We're taking the foetal monitor off now, Rachael.' Everything had been explained to her carefully, just as she'd asked. Long conversations with her obstetrician where he had gently suggested a Caesarean section, the safest option given her previous birth, and Rachael had agreed as long as every tiny detail was relayed to her, a small attempt to stay in control as she faced the scariest time of her life.

But suddenly she didn't want to hear Dr Carmody, didn't want to know the details. The only thing that mattered, the only sound Rachael wanted to hear was the sound of her baby's cries.

'Don't tell me any more,' Rachael said to the gentle eyes above the mask. 'I've changed my mind, I just want you to do it.'

She closed her eyes then held Hugh's hand tightly. She blocked out all the sounds that whirred around, waiting for just one. She felt a tugging and she felt Hugh move beside her, heard the wonder in his voice as he begged her to look.

'Rachael.'

The green screen that covered her abdomen was moving, a tiny angry, indignant face blinking, screwing up its little eyes as a wail filled the room.

'One angry baby.' Dr Carmody smiled, delivering the slippery bundle into the shaking arms of its mother. 'One happy mum,' he added, and the whole theatre tearoom would later hear that there had definitely been a tear in those eyes as Dr Carmody had clipped the cord.

'It's a boy.' Rachael was crying and laughing as the midwife rubbed him vigorously with a towel, skilfully wrapping the taut bundle of flesh into a swaddle and tucking them both in. 'He's OK?' she asked anxiously. 'Is he all right?'

'He's perfect,' the midwife said, then, because Rachael really needed to hear it, she said it again. 'He's just perfect.'

Rachael held him, cuddled him, loved him, not even letting him go when they stitched her up, just gazed at her new baby, her head resting by Hugh's as they marvelled at this most wonderful gift.

'The cord bank has been,' Dr Carmody said as he worked diligently on, 'they passed on their thanks.

Not many people donate the umbilical cord unfortunately. What made you think of it?'

Rachael looked up for the first time. 'We've got a friend, Kimbi,' she explained. 'She's got leukaemia but she's doing really well—she's actually in remission now.' She felt Hugh's arm tighten around her as she spoke. 'It was research that's gone into cord blood that ended up saving her.' She looked down at her new infant, her baby soft and safe in her arms, his little pink face nudging her breasts, and she thought her heart might burst with happiness. 'It's sort of our gift, our way of saying thank you. If that makes sense.'

'It makes perfect sense.'

It was the best day of her life. The room was filled with blue balloons, blue cards and arrangement after arrangement of blue, white and lilac flowers. Helen arrived, looking stunning as she did these days, crying unashamedly when she held the newborn. And when the last visitor had gone, when Hugh had kissed her goodnight, she lay back on the cool, crisp sheets, Harry's Perspex crib pushed up close beside her bed.

Leaning over, she gave her son a goodnight kiss on his soft warm cheek then kissed him once more for Hugh. And finally, with tears filling her eyes, she kissed him again.

For Amy.

'Room for one more in the bed?'

Hugh was back, a bottle of champagne in one hand, a pair of theatre blues in the other.

'It's past visiting time.' Wiping her cheeks

quickly, she pulled up the sheet. 'The midwives won't like it.'

'It was the midwives that suggested it.' He filled two glasses and handed one to her. 'They know a thing or three, those women. They said you might need a bit of a cuddle.'

She was about to say no, to push away the glass and remind him she was breastfeeding, but something in his eyes stopped her. Something told Rachael he needed this just as much as she did, that it wasn't the time to shut him out. 'The midwives were right,' she said softly.

The champagne was delicious, cold and icy and extremely well earned. 'Make sure no one comes in.' She watched as Hugh pulled off his clothes and with lightning speed changed into his blues and then climbed on the bed beside her.

'You look like you're settling in for the long haul,' Rachael murmured, her eyes heavy with sleep. 'Just how long did the midwives say you could stay for?'

'All night,' he whispered, pulling her into his arms. 'And the same again tomorrow. You're right, darling.' His arms wrapped tightly around her as she moulded herself to his body, placing the softest, gentlest kiss on her lips before resting her back on the pillow. 'I'm here for the long haul, and there's no place on earth I'd rather be.

'We're a family.'

Modern Romance™
...seduction and
passion guaranteed

Tender Romance™
...love affairs that
last a lifetime

Medical Romance™
...medical drama
on the pulse

Historical Romance™
...rich, vivid and
passionate

Sensual Romance™
...sassy, sexy and
seductive

Blaze Romance™
...the temperature's
rising

27 new titles every month.

Live the emotion

MILLS & BOON®

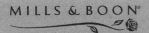

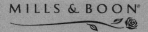

Medical Romance™

THE PREGNANT POLICE SURGEON
by Abigail Gordon

GP and local police surgeon Dr Imogen Rossiter is fiery, beautiful – and pregnant! When she meets fellow GP and police surgeon Dr Blair Nesbitt sparks fly between them…until Imogen tells him she is carrying another man's child. Both are thrown into an emotional turmoil that tests the strength of their love.

THE GPs' WEDDING by Barbara Hart

Dr Fabian Drumm and Dr Holly Westwood were happily planning their wedding – until Fabian's mother told him his real father was not the man he called 'Dad' and he had half-siblings in America! Fabian changes his mind about marriage and children – but Holly refuses to give him up!

HER ITALIAN DOCTOR by Jean Evans

Dr Beth Bryant is determined to find fault with her new boss – until she recognises him as the drop-dead gorgeous Italian she saw that morning on her way to work! Dr Nick D'Angelo spells sex appeal in the extreme, and his romantic intentions are glaring. But Beth doesn't want to feel the emotions of loving and losing again…

On sale 6th June 2003

Available at most branches of WH Smith, Tesco, Martins, Borders, Eason, Sainsbury's and all good paperback bookshops.

Don't miss *Book Ten* of this BRAND-NEW 12 book collection 'Bachelor Auction'.

Who says money can't buy love?

On sale 6th June

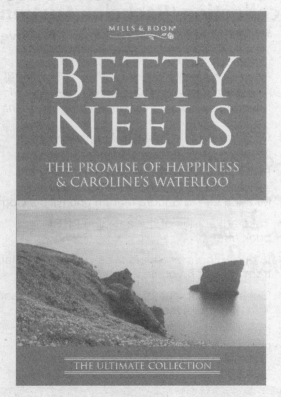

FREE!

2 Books
and a surprise gift!

We would like to take this opportunity to thank you for reading this Mills & Boon® book by offering you the chance to take TWO more specially selected titles from the Medical Romance™ series absolutely FREE! We're also making this offer to introduce you to the benefits of the Reader Service™—

- ★ FREE home delivery
- ★ FREE gifts and competitions
- ★ FREE monthly Newsletter
- ★ Books available before they're in the shops
- ★ Exclusive Reader Service discount

Accepting these FREE books and gift places you under no obligation to buy; you may cancel at any time, even after receiving your free shipment. Simply complete your details below and return the entire page to the address below. **You don't even need a stamp!**

YES! Please send me 2 free Medical Romance books and a surprise gift. I understand that unless you hear from me, I will receive 4 superb new titles every month for just £2.60 each, postage and packing free. I am under no obligation to purchase any books and may cancel my subscription at any time. The free books and gift will be mine to keep in any case.

M3ZEB

Ms/Mrs/Miss/Mr ....Initials..
BLOCK CAPITALS PLEASE

Surname...

Address...

....

....Postcode ....

Send this whole page to:
UK: The Reader Service, FREEPOST CN81, Croydon, CR9 3WZ
EIRE: The Reader Service, PO Box 4546, Kilcock, County Kildare (stamp required)